Meeting
Melanie

Also by Nancy Garden

Meeting & Melanie

Nancy Garden

Farrar Straus Giroux
New York

Library of Congress Cataloging-in-Publication Data
Garden, Nancy.
    Meeting Melanie / Nancy Garden.— 1st ed.
        p.   cm.
    Summary: Summer on her Maine island is enlivened for eleven-year-old
Allie when she befriends Melanie, a new girl with hidden talents and a
family secret that her mother is trying to hide.
    ISBN 0-374-34943-6
    [1. Friendship—Fiction.   2. Islands—Fiction.   3. Maine—Fiction.]
I. Title.

PZ7.G165 Me 2002
[Fic]—dc21
                                                                2002023884

For Frances Grossman,
with admiration, respect, and love.

My thanks to Eleanor Murphy, former
postmaster of West Tremont, Maine,
who very kindly checked the
manuscript for authenticity. Any
errors about island life that remain are
mine alone.

Meeting Melanie

One

Allie Ward's ma was string-thin and tired, her fingers raw from picking the meat out of crabs to sell in Spruce Harbor on the mainland across from the Wards' home on Seal Head Island, Maine. Allie's daddy had hurt his back in the spring and he'd had to lie in bed like, he said, "a beached whale," while his lobster traps sat in the yard, idle and empty, as they still were. No lobsters meant no money coming in, so now that school had closed for the summer, Daddy and Ma were sending Sarah and Matthew, Allie's little sister and brother, across to Aunt Eulalie's farm in Spruce Harbor to save on expenses. Aunt Hattie and Uncle Ted, who lived right down the road from the Wards, offered to take them, but Ma said if Sarah and Matthew were that near, they wouldn't understand why they couldn't come home. Allie was glad it was Aunt Eulalie they were going to; the other possibility, old Aunt Cora, would have been awful. Ma was never so tired that she didn't have a smile on her face or a squeeze or a cuddle for any of the three of them, and Eulalie was like that, too, but Allie knew Aunt Cora was so sour she'd turn pickles.

But it was some sad anyway that Sarah and Matthew had to go anywhere, even though it couldn't be helped. It couldn't be helped either that Allie'd have to spend a lot of the summer inside, helping Ma and Daddy "recoup," as Daddy put it. That sounded funny to Allie, like chicken coops, but what Daddy really meant was for Allie to help him and Ma start a pie-and-bread shop down on the town dock for the summer people and anyone else who wanted to buy. Of course most island women did their own baking, but as Ma said, "Everyone likes to get out of the kitchen now and then." Allie was going to help build shelves and a counter, and help sell once they got the whole thing going, plus mix up dough with Ma and knead it, pick berries for the pies, and pack the pies up for Daddy to deliver to the summer people's cottages. In between, Allie might baby-sit for the Corrigans, who were summer people, as she'd done before, and Ma would clean some summer people's cottages and maybe pick more crab, and they'd all pray that soon Daddy would be able to set his string again and go back to hauling traps.

But right now, while Ma was taking Sarah and Matthew across to Aunt Eulalie's, and Daddy was signing the papers that would let them make their shop out of the vacant room attached to the general store, Allie had nothing to do, so she climbed partway up the old pine tree near her house and hung upside down from it to see if she still could. It had been her favorite position when she was younger, but now her favorite was at the top, where the branches and trunk were thin and the tree swayed with her weight even when there wasn't any wind. From there she could gaze out beyond the harbor to the shimmering ocean, and be a pirate captain looking for victims, or a whaler looking for spouts.

Today, though, she stayed put only partway up, remembering how a couple of times last year she pretended to be a monkey, one of those little colobus monkeys her uncle Ted, who wrote travel articles for magazines, had seen in Africa. He and his son, Allie's cousin Dan, were the only people on the whole island to have gone so far away. Dan had been just about the most popular kid at Spruce Harbor High School because of his travels, at least according to his girlfriend, Katy Porter. Allie liked Dan—he was big and friendly like Uncle Ted—but he tended to tease and she knew he made up stuff sometimes, at least he had when she was little, telling her that there were tigers in the woods or that he'd seen sharks in the harbor. She liked Katy, who'd baby-sat her long ago and taught her to play jacks and how to do cat's cradle. Katy was pretty, too— "Prettiest girl on the island," Dan said, and Allie thought he was probably right.

"Chee-chee-chee-chee-chee!" Allie chattered as she had in last year's monkey-pretending days, scratching under her arms and feeling some old bored. Her two classmates, the only other island kids her age, which was almost twelve, Todd Gable and Michael Burns, had recently turned downright unfriendly, not wanting her to play with them anymore, though she was just as good as they were at rowing and playing ball and running and climbing. But now it was "Girls can't do this" and "Girls can't do that," even though she could, and better than they could, too, at times.

Why would a monkey chatter?

"Chee-chee-chee-chee-chee," Allie said again, as if saying it would tell her why. She heard a giggle under her, so she switched her head around and saw a girl standing there in fancy pressed shorts and a matching T-shirt that looked pressed, too—T-shirt poking out at the front more than Allie's poked out, though the girl didn't look any older.

"I can see your underpants," the girl said. "Yellow with blue flowers. What if a boy came along?"

Allie felt her face turn red. She flipped to a sitting position, thinking, *rotten baggy shorts!* She hated those underpants. They were the ones she waited to wear till all the others needed washing. Aunt Cora had given them to her.

Who did this fancy-looking girl with her pressed clothes think she was anyway?

Allie was ready to ignore her, climb higher, maybe, but then the girl smiled. It was a pretty smile, teeth without braces, sparkling white and even, and round cheeks puffing out rounder under blue eyes. Dimples, too.

"I'm sorry," the girl said. "That was a mean thing to say. They're pretty pants."

"I hate them," Allie said, still grumpy.

The girl smiled some more. "They don't quite go with the shorts. Or with climbing a tree."

Allie felt her face turn more red and again she cursed her shorts, which were faded tan and tattered around the hem. Who does this girl think she is, she thought once more. A princess or something? She wasn't a regular summer kid; none of the people who came every year had any kids her age, just younger ones like Betsy and Deirdre Corrigan. Last summer when she'd baby-sat them she'd shown them how to build fairy houses out of moss and sticks, and taken them rowing in Daddy's old skiff. That had been fun, but she'd had more fun with Todd and Michael.

Till they'd turned unfriendly.

Maybe the girl was just a bored tourist off today's mailboat, although it was only June and early for day-trippers.

"What's your name?" the girl asked.

"Allie Ward. What's yours?" she answered, half reluctant, half curious.

"Melanie Rochambeau. We're here for the summer."

Figures, Allie thought. Fancy name for a fancy person. Rochambeaus' was the big white house up on the hill, empty except for July and August and a week or two on either side of that. Nice old Mrs. Rochambeau had died last winter and there'd been rumors that her son had gotten the house and was bringing his family for the summer—

and sure enough, Allie'd heard that they'd arrived yester-day. Ma hadn't said anything about them, but Bill Hornby, who worked in the Rochambeaus' garden, said the young Mrs. R was hard as a half-tide ledge. Of course Bill Hornby was inclined to be grumpy when his arthritis was hurting him, which was most of the time, so one couldn't always count on his opinions.

Anyway, Allie knew she ought to say something, so she said, "Melanie's a pretty name." Well, it was. But fancy, too.

"I think it's dumb," Melanie said, and Allie looked closer, more interested. "My mother named me after someone in a book. *Gone With the Wind*. It's famous, about the Civil War. She named my big sister after the heroine. Mary Scarlett."

"That was the heroine's name?" Allie asked incredu-lously. "Mary Scarlett?"

Melanie shook her head. "Just Scarlett. But my grand-mother's name was Mary. Both my grandmothers." Melanie grinned. "At least she didn't name her Mary Mary."

"Yeah," said Allie, grinning back.

"What were you doing up there in the tree?"

"Nothing." Allie felt embarrassed again. "Just fooling around."

Melanie looked up at the pine's branches. "Teach me to climb? Please?"

"Sure," Allie said, astonished. Could there really be

someone who didn't know how to climb a tree? She scrambled down, and when she was standing beside Melanie, she saw that she, Allie, was taller, but not by much.

"My mother's kind of strict," Melanie explained. "She wants me and Mary Scarlett to be ladies all the time. I hate that. I hate it a lot."

"Well," said Allie, reaching up, "look. Put your hands on this branch, like this, one on each side. Then kind of walk up the trunk with your feet. Here, you watch."

By the time Melanie had gotten up in the tree, and Allie had joined her, and they were sitting side by side on twin branches, a shiny car—wicked red with spoke wheels—came roaring along the bumpy broken-up tar road outside Allie's house. A woman who looked almost too old for her girlish vivid blond pageboy hairdo leaned out and called "Melanie!" with her pink lipsticked mouth.

Melanie groaned. "That's my mother. I'd better go."

"Come back again," Allie said, though she hadn't meant to. "Here." She gave Melanie a hand, helping her swing down.

"You mean it?" Melanie looked up at her, blue eyes serious.

"Yeah," Allie said. "I do."

Two

Supper was down the road at Aunt Hattie and Uncle Ted's, "to celebrate signing the papers for the shop," Aunt Hattie said, dishing out mashed potatoes, but Allie was aware that it was because Ma was away and Aunt Hattie knew Allie and Daddy couldn't cook worth beans.

Uncle Ted, home for a while waiting to hear where his next writing assignment would send him, reached for the spoon when Aunt Hattie was done and plopped more potatoes on his plate. He was a big bear of a man, with a thick brown beard that made him look even more bearish than his solid round body. Allie couldn't understand what made him want to stay away from the island so much, although she had to admit that seeing monkeys and other things in faraway places must be pretty interesting. Still, she'd never been able to imagine anyplace better than home, where everyone knew everyone and the sky and the sea were almost like people, with different moods and quirks.

"Dan? John?" Uncle Ted said now, turning first to his

son, big and solid like him, and then to Allie's daddy, thin and pale, with his face creased with new wrinkles, because of the pain in his back, Allie figured. "Don't hold back if you want more."

Allie's daddy laughed. "You fixing to fatten me up for the slaughter, Ted?" he asked. "Hattie's already given me more than a man could decently eat. Most men, anyway," he said, with a wink at his sister-in-law.

No one, Allie noticed, wanting more potatoes herself, worries about me or Aunt Hattie having enough.

Aunt Hattie, almost as round as her husband, laughed good-naturedly and pushed a platter of fried haddock toward Allie's daddy. "Here, John. Ted's right about fattening you. Got to keep your strength up." She turned to Allie. "Maybe you'll hear from Mumma tonight," she said kindly, as if she knew Allie was missing her, which she was. The only other times Ma had been off-island overnight without Allie was to give birth, first to Sarah, who was eight years old now, and then, three years later, to Matthew.

"*Ma*, you mean," said Dan. "Allie doesn't call Aunt Cindy *Mumma* anymore. She's too grown-up for that. Right, Allie?"

Allie squirmed and nodded. You couldn't always tell when Dan was teasing and when he wasn't. Teasing, she figured, this time.

"Well," Aunt Hattie said, "I bet she thinks it sometimes. Dan, did you take that big box from off the mailboat up to Rochambeaus' yet?"

Allie pricked up her ears.

Dan speared a piece of haddock with his fork and shoved it into his mouth, nodding. "Yup," he said when he'd swallowed. "Full of clothes, I think. That woman— whew! She makes me shiver! Gave me a tip, though."

"Old Mrs. Rochambeau always did that, too," said Uncle Ted.

"Yeah, but old Mrs. Rochambeau gave a lot more of one. This one's nothing like her. Got a pretty daughter, though." Dan reached for the pickles, the end of the ones Ma and Allie had made last summer from cucumbers from Aunt Eulalie's farm. Allie and Daddy had brought the cukes over long before his back gave out, along with summer squash, corn, and enough beans, it seemed like, to feed half the island. There were still some left, too, lined up in jars down cellar.

Uncle Ted gave Dan a look. "You better not go getting any ideas about summer folks's daughters," he said. "What would Katy think?"

"Did I say anything?" Dan made his eyes look wide and innocent. "But she *is* some pretty. Long silky blond hair and a little turned-up nose and the prettiest mouth. Couldn't see much of her figure, though; she had on this sort of smock thing that covered her . . ."

"Dan!" Uncle Ted remonstrated, nodding toward Allie.

". . . whole body," Dan said, winking at Allie. "Maybe I'll just go up once in a while, see if they need anything."

"And maybe you won't," grunted Uncle Ted. "Would

someone like to give up custody of those peas for a few minutes?"

For most of the rest of the meal, the adults talked about what the papers Daddy had signed said about the new pie business using the room off the general store, and about using the big ovens in the Dockside Restaurant next door. After a while, Allie tuned out. She wondered what it was going to be like, working in a store. Ma and Daddy had promised she wouldn't have to work all the time, just sometimes, when they needed a hand. But still, it was going to be a big change, that was sure as tides.

After supper Allie helped Aunt Hattie with the dishes. Dan went off to visit Katy, so he must've been kidding about that Rochambeau girl—Melanie's sister, Mary Scarlett, Allie figured. Daddy and Uncle Ted sat outside and talked.

"It'll be a strange summer for you, Allie," Aunt Hattie allowed, swishing plates in soapy water. "But you're going to be a big help to Mumma and Daddy. I hope you know how grateful they are."

"I do, I guess," Allie said. She rubbed a plate vigorously. "I just wish Sarah and Matty hadn't had to go off."

"I know." Aunt Hattie sighed. "But they'll be better off on the farm. They'll have a good time there, Allie."

Allie shook her head. "Sarah'll cry after Mumma leaves them," she said. "She didn't want to go. And I bet Matty'll cry, too."

"Honey"—Aunt Hattie put her soapy hands on Allie's

shoulders—"you're right. They're little kids and they probably will cry their first night or two away from home. But you know what?"

Allie shook her head, fighting tears herself.

"Most likely they'll be fine after a week. There's so much to do on a farm, so much that'll be new to them— why, they'll come back full of adventures to tell about, and they'll probably cry once they're back, too, missing the farm. That's how little kids are."

"Some little kids," Allie said stubbornly. "Not Sarah."

"Well, I guess you know your sister better than I do." Aunt Hattie turned back to the dishes. "But people are full of surprises. Why, when I was Sarah's age, I had to go off-island, too. I was sick and I had to go miles away to a big hospital in Bangor, then even farther away, to Boston. Lordy, was I scared! My mumma came with me, but she couldn't stay, and I was some old homesick when she left. But after a while, I got used to it and I even liked some of it, not the things the doctors had to do, but the other kids and the nurses. I guess if a little kid could like that, she could like anything."

"Maybe," said Allie, but, she thought, Sarah is Sarah and Aunt Hattie is Aunt Hattie. People aren't the same.

Later, walking home with Daddy under a starry sky with a fresh salty breeze off the water, Allie said, "If Mumma doesn't call us, can we call her at Aunt Eulalie's and see how Sarah and Matty are?"

"Well, I guess we *could*." Daddy curled his big hand around Allie's. It was smoother than usual now that he hadn't been hauling traps; Allie missed the roughness. "But we probably shouldn't. It's a long-distance call, and your ma'll want to call Aunt Eulalie herself when she gets back, to see how Sarah and Matty take being without her. You can talk to them then, Chipmunk, okay?"

Allie smiled past her disappointment and snuggled against her father's side. "Chipmunk" was his special name for her, though he hadn't used it for a while. He had one for each of them. Sarah was "Turtle" because she was shy and quiet, and Matthew was "Owl" or "Owlet" because he'd been a very solemn baby.

"Okay."

They walked on in silence, Allie enjoying his closeness and having him all to herself for once. He'd been brave, having to lie flat on his back for so long. She knew he'd been wicked bored, so she'd read to him every day after school when he wasn't listening to the Red Sox on the radio. "Thank goodness for baseball," Ma had said more than once that awful spring.

He was better now that he was up and around, though he walked slowly, still, and crooked like an old man when his back hurt. It could get bad again anytime, Dr. Coolidge over to Spruce Harbor had said, but Daddy was determined to go back out on his boat, and so he tried to be careful, and he did his exercises faithfully every other morning. They'd help, Dr. Coolidge had said, to make his back well and strong. But if it did get bad again, he'd warned, Daddy'd probably have to go back to the big hospital in Bangor for an operation. Allie shuddered, thinking of that, for that would be risky, Dr. Coolidge had told them, and there was a chance Daddy might not be able to walk afterward.

Awful, that was. Too awful to think about.

"Daddy?"

"Hmm?"

"What'll we do if the pie shop doesn't work?"

"It'll work, Chipmunk. We'll make it work, you and Mumma and I, with Dan's help."

"Yes, but what if it doesn't? What if no one wants the pies or the bread or what if there aren't enough berries?"

Daddy stopped and turned to face her. "I never saw anyone on this whole island who wouldn't practically kill for one of Mumma's pies. And all signs point to a good year for berries." He tousled her hair, then bent down, looking closely at her. "If it doesn't work, Allie, we'll think of something else. And if it turns out I can't haul traps, I'll try another kind of work. I could learn something new—I'm not an old dog yet. There's all kinds of jobs on the mainland. And it might not be so bad, living there."

"The mainland!" said Allie, horrified. "But we can't live there!"

"What an island girl you are," her father said, tousling her hair again.

That put her in mind to ask him about the thing she'd

been thinking about ever since he'd been laid up. It had never been the right time, but maybe now, with the two of them walking home together like old friends and the night falling softly around them, maybe now would be a good time.

"Daddy?"

"Hmm?"

"Daddy?" she said again, stepping around in front of him so he'd have to stop walking. "I've got this idea I've been having for a while. About how I could help more than in the shop."

He looked down at her, his brown eyes soft and loving and serious. "What's that, my Chipper?" "Chipper" was short for Chipmunk and even more special.

"Well, Uncle Ted let you give Dan his first string of lobster traps when he was twelve, remember?"

"I do indeed," Daddy said. "But . . ."

"And that's when most boys start lobstering, at least a little."

"That's true, Allie, but . . ."

"And I'm as strong as Todd and Michael; I can even beat Michael arm wrestling. And I can row faster and longer than both of them in Todd's peapod and in our old skiff, too. And I've helped you haul traps twice now, and I know how. So . . ."

Daddy knelt down and put his hands around Allie's skinny waist. "No," he said gently. "No."

"But Daddy, look, the way I figure it, I could spend a

month or two just doing traps in close to shore, like Todd and Michael do, and like Dan did when he started. And then gradually I could go out farther. I know I couldn't tend all the traps you tend, but I could at least get us some lobsters, enough to eat and a few to sell, and that would help with the money. Please, Daddy, please?"

Daddy bowed his head and squeezed her waist with his big hands. Then he pushed himself up to his feet, wincing and touching his back for a second as he rose. Allie winced with him. He pulled Allie to him in a hug, smoothing her shaggy hair—she herself had cut it—and stroking her shoulders. "Sweet Allie," he said, "you are the very best daughter any man could have. And I know you're as strong as those boys and twice as willing. But I've put my traps up for the summer and settled inside myself about it, and if I sent you out, Mumma and I would lose so much sleep worrying, we'd turn gray before our time. Sweet Allie, you're a girl and there's no real reason in the world why a good strong girl like you couldn't set a string and haul as well as any boy your age. But that'll change soon, for you're going to turn into a woman, like it or not, and women just plain aren't as strong as men. No point in your getting all excited about lobstering just to have to give it up."

"But Daddy, that's not fair!"

"Maybe not, Chipper, but that's how it is. Tell you what, though."

"What?" Allie said, her voice tight and muffled, choking back tears. There was the plan she'd mulled over for weeks, gone in a few seconds. It *wasn't* fair, and nothing he could say could change that, except if he changed his mind.

But she knew her daddy, and she knew he wouldn't.

"You can help me and Dan tomorrow building counters for the shop . . ."

"You already said I could do that!"

". . . and soon as I can, I'll start teaching you to drive the old Jeep, and if you take to it like you've taken to boats, one of your other jobs this summer can be delivering pies and bread. How's that?"

She tried to put lobstering aside long enough to think about it.

It wasn't as good as hauling traps would be, but it was pretty good. And she'd been wanting to learn to drive, too. Neither Todd nor Michael could yet, as far as she knew. They'd shut up their teasing, maybe, if she could.

"Maybe," she said cautiously. "Promise you'll let me if I learn?"

"Yes, I promise. Cross my heart." He made the gesture so grandly and with such a solemn face that Allie laughed.

"Even though I'm not even close to sixteen?"

"Pooh! On here no one worries about that, and well you know it. But if I catch you driving on the mainland when you go there to school in two years, I'll—I'll . . ."

She grinned. "You'll what?" Daddy'd made some wicked elaborate threats in his time, but he'd never carried any of them out.

"I'll think of something," he said, and they walked on, with Allie feeling a bit happier.

Later, though, when she'd brushed her teeth and washed her face and put on her pajamas, she realized she was still left with what he'd said they'd do if none of their plans worked, so she crept downstairs and found him sitting in Gran's old rocking chair that Aunt Eulalie had sent over from the farm "because it was like the one President John F. Kennedy used when his back was bad."

"Daddy?"

"Still up, Chipper? You'd best get some sleep. Don't want any banged thumbs or cut-off fingers working on those shelves tomorrow."

"It's just—well, did you mean it about getting a job on the mainland if the pies don't work out? Us moving there?"

He sighed. "I'm not counting on that happening," he said. "But if it does, well, yes, I guess we might have to think about moving."

"We belong here," Allie protested. *I don't want to go off-island ever, except maybe for visits; not even to school in two years,* she wanted to add. But she figured she'd best keep that to herself for a while.

"I don't want to move, Allie. And like I said, I'm not counting on that happening. But if it's what we have to do, it's what we'll do. The main thing is for us to find a way to get by." He squeezed her shoulders, hugging her. "Right?"

"Right," she managed to squeak, even though it really wasn't.

It took her a long time to fall asleep that night.

Move!

Allie couldn't think of anything much worse.

Three

"It'll look better in the morning" was what Ma'd always told her when Allie went to bed chewing on a problem. And, Allie thought the next day, rubbing sandpaper along the wooden counter Dan and Daddy had just finished putting up across the back of the pie-shop-to-be, Ma's right. The sun was shining as if it, at least, didn't have a care in the world, and through the open window Allie could see it sparkling on the water and glinting off someone's green wire traps, piled up and waiting on one corner of the town dock. The only lobster boat in the harbor was Daddy's, waiting, too; the others had already been out for hours, but Dan's small sloop and a few dinghies bobbed gently on their moorings—and before Allie turned back to what she'd been doing, Michael and Todd passed by in Todd's dad's skiff. "Hey," Allie shouted, sticking her head out the window. "Where are you off to?"

"Big Hog Island," Todd called back. "Don't you wish you could come?"

"With you two?" Allie shouted. "I'd sooner drown!"

And that, Allie Ward, she said to herself, going back to her sanding, is a sure-enough lie. At least there's no sign of their lobstering yet.

"Looks nice, Allie," Daddy said, coming back inside from where he and Dan had been cutting lumber for shelves, and running his big hand over the surface of the counter. "You're a good sander. But here." He handed her a fresh piece of sandpaper. "That old scrap you're using's just about done for. I sure wish that power sander of Clarence's was working!"

Clarence was Clarence Fitz, the elderly retired fisherman who ran the general store. He'd offered Daddy and Dan the use of his tools, but Daddy said most of them were just about as old as Clarence's great-grandfather would be if he were still alive.

"It's okay," Allie said. "I like it this way." She pulled the worn sandpaper out of the grooves on the metal hand sander she'd been using and fitted the new piece in. "Don't have to choke on sawdust like they do over to the boat shop all the time."

"And no tingling arm or ringing ears afterwards," agreed her father. "I guess you're right. Still, it'd go quicker with the power one." He looked at his watch. "Mailboat's due in an hour. Wonder if Mumma'll be on it."

"Sure hope so," Allie said.

Daddy and Dan had put up several shelves by the time the mailboat whistled, and Daddy decided they could all take an hour off to eat the lunches he and Allie had made for them—peanut butter sandwiches, with the last of Ma's strawberry jam. They went out onto the dock to meet the boat before they ate and watched two summer families and a bunch of neighbors scramble off, but there was no sign of Ma. Then George Jenks, captain of the mailboat, heaved the big lumpy sack of letters and magazines and newspapers and packages ashore and Ginny Nichols, the postmistress, loaded it up in her rusty rattletrap of a Ford car and drove off with it.

Just as Allie was turning away, missing Ma but thinking about those sandwiches, a strong female voice called out, "Careful with those canvases, George, for pity's sake!" Allie turned back, a smile already stretching the corners of her mouth, and sure enough, there was Miss Letty Feathergill, island-born nurse and amateur artist, retired and wintering far away in Boston, back for the summer with her paintboxes and brushes and probably a few fresh bandages and splints and whatnot to replenish the island's medical supplies.

"Now don't fuss, dear," George said, handing Miss Feathergill ashore and winking at Daddy as Allie and the others on the dock swarmed forward to greet her. "You know I wouldn't drop 'em—uh-oh!" Everyone gasped as George, pretending disaster, dipped the flat oblong bundle near the water and yanked it up just in time.

"Should know better than to trust you, George," Miss Feathergill said, punching his arm playfully. "Still up to your old tricks, I see." She threw her arms wide, as if including all of them plus the island itself in a huge embrace—and it looked to Allie as if she would and could, even though her natural smallness was made smaller by the neat blue skirt suit and flowered blouse she wore, incongruously topped off by a red-and-white bandana tied askew over her wispy gray hair. "Oh, I'm glad to be home!" she exclaimed to everyone, then cried eagerly, "John!" as she stepped forward and hugged Daddy. "How's the back? Poor lamb, what a nuisance—and Dan"—she pumped his hand—"my, you've become a handsome devil." At last she turned to Allie, spreading her arms again, and Allie rushed into them, breathing in the faint soapy scent that Miss Feathergill always had about her, even when she also smelled of turpentine or linseed oil, or antiseptic, or even fresh dirt—for Miss Feathergill kept up an extensive garden when she wasn't painting or teaching others to draw and paint, or helping out with medical emergencies if there was no nurse or doctor on the island. There wasn't either now, hadn't been since March. "Allie, my dear, I've missed you. Wait'll you see the seeds I've brought!"

As Miss Feathergill turned away, greeting each person on the dock by name and giving each a warm personal message, Dan moved off with his lunch bag, and Daddy, handing Allie hers, answered Allie's unspoken question by saying, "Yes, you may help Miss Feathergill take her things up to her house, but be back by one or soon after"—and he followed Dan.

So while Miss Feathergill finished her greetings, Allie

got the old wheelbarrow out of harbor master Billy Clasp's shed and piled Miss Feathergill's luggage onto it, heaving the suitcases up with one hand and lifting the boxes with a flourish, in case Daddy was looking.

But he wasn't.

Then she stood beside the wheelbarrow, holding her lunch bag and waiting for Miss Feathergill to finish her hellos, which took a long time since word had traveled fast that she'd arrived and lots more people had run down to the dock to greet her. But at last Miss Feathergill broke free and, shouldering her large straw pocketbook and carrying her big wooden paint box—"home of the tools of one of my trades," as she called it—she beckoned to Allie. Together they trudged along the gently curving uphill street to the tiny gray shingled house that Miss Feathergill's parents had built and where Miss Feathergill had spent her first thirteen years, plus weekends and vacations for the next four while she was in high school off-island in Spruce Harbor. She'd been home just for vacations after that, when she was in nursing school in New York and, later, when she'd worked in one big hospital or another. For the last two years, though, since she'd retired, she'd talked of moving back to the island year round. "And I will, too," she assured Allie when Allie brought it up again as they approached the house. "I've just got to clear up some more things in Boston before I do. You can't imagine what a tangle life can become after sixty-seven years. Whew!" She stepped back after pushing open the unlocked door. "Talk about musty! Let's get some air in here!" Miss Feathergill flew about the house flinging windows open. Allie helped her with the stuck ones. "Now the studio," she said when the main part was being well aired. She pulled open the door to the small addition she'd put on the house after she'd worked off-island for a few years—windows all around and a skylight in the roof, and her big easel standing ready in the middle of the floor. An old zinc sink from a dump on the mainland stood in one corner, and the walls supported counters and cupboards and shelves galore. It made Allie want to be an artist, that room—not that she'd really decided yet what she wanted to be, except she thought it might have something to do with lobstering. Anyway, despite the drawing lessons Miss Feathergill had given her and other island kids now and then, in Allie's opinion she herself didn't have any artistic talent worth thinking about.

"That's better," said Miss Feathergill. "Now, let me just see about some tea." She rummaged in one of the boxes she'd brought with her and pulled out a flowered tin canister and a box of powdered milk. "This'll have to do till the fridge gets going," she said, closing the small refrigerator's door, left open to prevent mold while it was unused; she flipped its switch on. "And you can tell me everything that's happened since last September. With any luck, Clarence will have started the water up." She went to the sink and tentatively turned the faucet, out of which came a thin rusty stream, soon thickening and then clearing as the electric pump whirred outside. "Bless him." She filled her battered aluminum kettle, lit the stove, and sat down. "Oh, leave that," she said, for Allie had put down her lunch bag and started to put groceries away. "What I want is the news." She grasped Allie's hand. "How is your father, really?" she asked anxiously.

"He'll be all right, I think." Allie let herself be pulled down into the chair where she'd sat often every summer for as long as she could remember, sometimes to have a skinned knee bathed and painted with Mercurochrome, or a tear-stained face gently washed if there'd been a crisis, usually involving Todd and Michael. "It hurts him some, still, but we're opening a pie shop." She filled Miss Feathergill in on that, and then, while they drank their tea, she added what she knew of the new group of Rochambeaus— and soon it was past one o'clock and time to go back to the shop.

"You keep me posted," Miss Feathergill called after her as Allie ran down the hill, trying to eat her till-then-ignored sandwich on the way. "And tell your mumma I'll take the first pie she bakes if it's not already spoken for."

Four

"*It's a good thing* you're on the tall side," Daddy said early the next morning as he adjusted the driver's seat of the old Jeep for Allie after she'd served him a not-very-successful breakfast of hard fried eggs and almost-burned toast.

Allie grunted. She'd found that she could reach the pedals well enough if she stretched in one direction, and she could see out if she stretched in the other, but she had to admit that she fit a lot better when Daddy had finished with the seat.

"Okay." Daddy folded his long body into the Jeep. "Now. Here's the key. Step down on the clutch—that's this pedal"—he pointed—"and the brake—that one—and turn the key."

Allie did, and after a second the engine made a sound like a young harbor seal's bark, and turned over.

Allie grinned.

So did Daddy, and he patted her shoulder. "Well done.

You're a smart pupil. Now figure out where you're going to go."

"Huh?"

"Doesn't make any sense to start up aimlessly. You wouldn't start rowing before you knew where you were headed, would you?"

Allie shook her head, though she knew she had, sometimes.

"Well, then? Where are we off to?"

"Um—maybe up by school?"

"Good choice—but hold on a sec, Chipmunk, I forgot something. Turn 'er off again—just keep your feet on the clutch and the brake and twist the key the other way. Right. Now, let me show you the gears . . ."

After about ten minutes of showing her how to shift into first, second, third, and reverse, and explaining what each gear was for, Daddy finally piloted Allie out of the driveway and onto the bumpy road, where she made the old Jeep groan up the hill to school. The Jeep pitched and yawed over the potholes and bits of torn-up macadam like a peapod on a stormy sea, but Allie felt as proud as if she'd captained the mailboat when she passed Todd and Michael and managed to honk the horn and wave. They stared, openmouthed, as she turned into the schoolyard—tried to turn, that is, but she veered left when she should've gone right, until Daddy reached over and grabbed the wheel, turning it the opposite way. "It's a car, not Dan's sloop," he said. "The wheel's a wheel, not a tiller. You want her to go right, you turn the wheel right, Allie."

Sheepishly, Allie nodded, and managed to stop close to smoothly, with her feet on the clutch and brake again.

"And never mind waving and honking and gawking till you get the hang of what you're doing," he added severely, but with a twinkle in his eye that told Allie he knew why she'd felt so triumphant. "Good job, though, except for that," he said, patting her shoulder. "But we'd best head back down to the shop now. Mumma will be home for sure today, and we've got to finish up those cupboards and sweep the place out. Well, what's keeping you?"

"You mean I'm driving to the shop?" Allie asked, amazed.

"I don't know why not. Here I am, in a perfectly good Jeep, with a perfectly good driver. Seems to me I wouldn't have much more brain than a clam if I decided to walk."

Carefully, Allie shifted into reverse.

All morning, Allie helped Dan and Daddy build the last cupboard and fit it into place. It was a fancy one with wide, deep shelves, to show off the pies. "We'll get glass doors for it, maybe, when we make some money," Daddy said, stepping back to view it as Allie finished sanding and Dan opened the can of stain. "Clear Walnut," it was called; Daddy said it would be dark enough to set off the pies nicely, as long as they weren't burned, which Allie knew they wouldn't be with Ma making them.

"How come you want glass doors?" said Allie. "It looks good just as it is."

"Keep the flies off," Daddy said—"and here's Mumma, I bet," he added as the mailboat whistled.

They all ran out on the dock, and Allie climbed up on one of the pilings, wrapping her legs around it and perching. She watched the mailboat round one of the two arms of land that came out from the island, embracing the harbor and making it a natural shelter. Watching the mailboat come in was one thing she'd never tired of, even in all the years she'd done it. Most everybody on the island lived by its schedule in one way or another, coming down to the dock to meet it if someone or something was coming, or, if they wanted their mail right away, marking the time the boat came and adding on to it the time it would take Ginny Nichols to get the mail up to the tiny post office next to her house, plus the time it would probably take her to sort it.

No one was a more faithful mailboat meeter than odd-looking Johnny Buttons, and Allie nodded to him now as he came and stood next to her, a tallish figure with an apologetic stance, like a nun buoy tipped by a rolling sea, and a face that, as Ma said, "only a mother could love." Johnny had been born with a flat squashed nose and a big mouth in the shape of a tipped-over *D*. His own parents had died when he was small, and he'd gone on the town, with the selectmen looking after his welfare and everyone making sure he had food and clothes. Even though Daddy and some of the other men took Johnny their old clothes before they were worn out, Johnny still seemed to wear the same pants and the same plaid flannel shirt winter and summer. Every so often, one of the men would take Johnny into the cabin he lived in and scrub him down under the shower.

And right now, Allie couldn't help but notice, Johnny was about due for another sluicing. But she said, "Morning, Johnny," anyway, and Johnny gave her the odd sideways look that was his regular greeting and said something that sounded like "Mawn." Johnny didn't talk much, and when he did it was hard to tell what he said, but he could play tunes on a comb wrapped with paper and he'd read every book in the town library and in the schoolhouse, plus every book and newspaper that folks on the island gave or lent him. He knew every corner of the island better than most people, too, and Allie had heard Miss Feathergill say more than once that he'd be a good guide for the tourists if only he could communicate more clearly.

But Allie'd developed a kind of sign language with Johnny over the years and they'd "discussed" *Lad: A Dog* and *My Friend Flicka* and *Hans Brinker, or The Silver Skates* enough to let Allie know that he liked them all and that he knew most books are either sad or scary in the middle or toward the end and then cheer up. "I don't think he's dumb like some people say," she told Ma. "I think he just can't get the words out."

"Have you seen those new people up to Rochambeaus'?" Allie asked Johnny now as he stood there next to her perch playing "Boston Come-All-Ye" on his comb while they both watched the mailboat make her way along the channel. "I've met one of them, and she seems nice, but I guess her mother isn't."

Johnny made a grunting noise and nodded, so Allie figured he'd seen them, too.

"Did you see Mrs. Rochambeau yesterday?" she asked. "I mean the young one, not the one that died." She laughed at the idea of seeing old Mrs. Rochambeau's ghost, and Johnny's mouth twitched as he grunted again, short rhythmic sounds this time, which Allie knew added up to laughter. "Dan says the young one's kind of stiff."

"Uh UP," Johnny said.

"Stuck up," Allie repeated, pretty sure that that was what he'd meant. "Yes."

The mailboat whistled again, and both of them concentrated on watching her ease smoothly into her berth alongside the dock. Daddy and Dan came out of the shop and Clarence Fitz came out of the general store, wiping his hands on the grayish-white butcher's apron he wore when he cleaned and cut up fish. Ginny Nichols drove up, and out of the corner of her eye Allie saw the Corrigan children, Betsy and Deirdre, tearing down the road. "Allie! Allie!" they shrieked, running to her and shoving Johnny Buttons aside as they grabbed at her legs, almost knocking her off her perch.

"Hi!" Allie jumped off the piling and caught Deirdre,

whose momentum nearly sent her into the water. "Say excuse me to Mr. Buttons."

Deirdre, who was five, looked sourly at Johnny, and Betsy, who was only a year older, stared.

"Go on," said Allie severely. "You bumped into him."

" 'Scuse me," Deirdre said petulantly, and then in a loud whisper, not at all disguised by the hand she held sideways to her mouth, she said to Allie, "He's scary."

"No, he's not," Allie told her as Johnny moved off. "That's just looks. He's just different from other folks. Did you come yesterday?"

"Yes, on the last boat, late," said Betsy. "Deirdre was asleep."

"I was not!" Deirdre protested indignantly.

"Were too!"

"Does it matter?" Allie asked them, stopping the shouting match before it really got going, as she'd learned to do last summer.

"Are you going to take care of us this summer?" Betsy asked.

"Sure," Allie said, watching the boat. "If your mumma wants me to. And if I have time. We're opening a store," she explained. "A pie shop. Right over there." She pointed.

"I don't see a store," said Betsy.

"It's not open yet. You'll see it when it is, and . . ." Allie broke off, spotting her mother at the rail of the mailboat; she gave each child a quick hug. "There's my ma," she said. "I've got to go meet her. See you later, alligator."

"After a while, crocodile!" both children chorused, giggling.

Ma, Allie could see as she moved to the edge of the dock, looked just as tired as she had when she'd left. She let Mr. Jenks hand her out, which was something she never did—and what were those bags he was swinging ashore for her? It was obvious they were hers, for she was watching as if she were scared he'd drop them or bruise whatever was inside.

"Ma!" Allie shouted, running to her.

Ma smiled and opened her arms, folding Allie in a warm soft hug that made Allie realize even more than before how much she'd missed her.

"Allie," she said. "I see you kept your daddy alive." She looked up, her smile growing as Daddy hugged her. With one arm around his wife and the other around Allie, he turned as if to steer them away from the boat.

But Ma stopped him. "Wait, John," she said. "I've brought some berries from Eulalie for the pies and some things that young Mrs. Rochambeau ordered which I promised we'd deliver to her."

Daddy raised his eyebrows, and Allie looked up at Ma's weary face, ready to be mad that young Mrs. Rochambeau had made her do errands for her.

"I forgot to tell you," Ma said to Daddy. "She arranged it the day she came, when I was up there finishing cleaning. It's those bags there." Ma pointed to two big canvas shopping bags standing on the dock next to her paper one, her small suitcase, and the two big boxes of strawberries Mr. Jenks was just now setting down next to them.

"That's the lot, I think," Mr. Jenks said. "You sure travel light, Cindy."

"Oh, I know," Ma said, chuckling. "Seems to me I must've forgotten something, don't you think?"

"If you have, I'll just swim over for it." Mr. Jenks hopped aboard again.

"I knew you would, George, I knew you would." Ma turned back to Daddy, snuggling under his arm and sighing. "It's good to be home."

"You look tired, Cin," Daddy said fondly. "I'll just run you up to the house in the Jeep."

Allie looked at him hopefully, but he shook his head and she stepped back. "You could maybe get those bags up to Mrs. Rochambeau," he said to her. "In the wheelbarrow."

Allie nodded, disappointed on the one hand but pleased on the other. Maybe she'd see Melanie again!

Five

One bag was heavy—it had books in it, Ma said—and the other, containing what seemed to be wrapped-up sheets and towels, was less so, so the old wheelbarrow tended to tip as Allie trundled up the hill. The weight and the uneven load made the trip take longer than she'd thought it would, and by the time she got to the fancy wrought-iron gate in front of the big white house, her muscles were aching and her stomach was grumbling, for it was way past lunchtime.

For a moment she stood uncertainly outside the gate, remembering how old Mrs. Rochambeau had always left it open. But it was closed now, and Allie couldn't figure out what to do. There didn't seem to be any kind of bell, and she wasn't sure she should just open it and barge in—if she even could; it looked wicked heavy. But then she spotted Bill Hornby scuttling toward her.

"Allie Ward," Mr. Hornby barked, his ruddy, weather-beaten face very red, and Allie figured he was having one of his bad days. "What do you think you're doing up here?"

"Delivering this stuff," Allie said, indicating the bags.

Mr. Hornby surveyed the wheelbarrow's load doubtfully. "And what might that be?"

"I dunno," Allie told him. "I think one's books and the other's sheets and towels."

"That barrow's none too clean," Mr. Hornby said severely.

Allie looked at it sheepishly. She hadn't thought of that. Neither, apparently, had Daddy when he'd told her to use it.

Mr. Hornby sighed. "Young Mrs. Rochambeau's mighty persnickety," he said gloomily. "I don't doubt she'll be some mad if those bags are muddied. You should've swept the dirt out. Why you young 'uns don't *think* is beyond me!"

Allie bit her tongue so she wouldn't say anything rude.

Mr. Hornby shook his head in an exasperated way as he swung the gate open. "Come on, then. You'd better take 'em to her yourself, dirt and all."

"They aren't *that* dirty," Allie couldn't help saying, even though Ma had said one should be patient with Mr. Hornby and sorry for him because of his arthritis. She pushed the barrow through the gate and then turned. "That girl Melanie wouldn't be around, would she?"

Bill Hornby shrugged as he swung the gate closed

again. "I wouldn't know. She darts all over the place. Undisciplined, if you ask me."

I *don't*, Allie retorted silently, and she continued up the wide gravel drive, vowing to look for Melanie if she could. The drive was lined with flower beds on both sides—red poppies and white daisies and blue lupines and yellow and purple and maroon flowers Allie didn't recognize and couldn't name.

The white house stood sideways to the driveway, its long, low two-story shape curving gently as the drive curved. Smack-dab in the middle, between windows marching right and left on either side, was a heavy black door with a bright brass knocker in its center. To the right, across the curve of the driveway, rose a white clapboard garage made to look like an old-fashioned coach house.

Allie stepped up to the door of the main house and knocked.

She knocked again.

A pleasant-looking stout woman in a black dress and a white pinafore-type apron opened the door. "Yes?" she said, her eyes blank except for surprise as they looked down at Allie.

Allie felt like she was in a movie. Old Mrs. Rochambeau had come to the door herself when she'd invited Allie and her parents to tea once. She'd also always greeted everyone on the Fourth of July, when all the islanders and summer people were invited to watch fireworks from the terraced lawns in back of the house. Allie wondered if they'd be invited to do that this year.

"Hi." Allie stuck out her hand and then pulled it back, thinking maybe that wasn't what you were supposed to do when a servant opened someone's front door. "I'm Allie Ward. Mrs. Ward's daughter?" She paused, but the woman was still looking at her blankly. "Cindy Ward? She cleans this house most Fridays in the summer. She cleaned here a few days ago, getting ready for the Rochambeaus to come."

The woman brightened at last, as if relieved to learn that maybe Allie had a good reason to be standing there. "Oh, yes," she said. "Cindy." She looked down at the wheelbarrow. "What have we here?"

"Mrs. Rochambeau asked my mother to bring these bags for her on the mailboat," Allie explained, deciding not to mention the dirt, which in any case didn't seem to have stuck all that much to the bags. "I don't know any more than that, except Ma's tired so Daddy asked me to bring them up. Um—is Melanie around?" she added quickly, for the woman had already stooped, picking up the lighter of the two bags.

"I think she's resting on the porch," said the woman.

"Could I see her?"

The woman gave her an odd look. "I doubt it," she said. "But I could ask her mother."

Quickly, Allie weighed her chances. She remembered

what Melanie and everyone else had said about young Mrs. Rochambeau, and she decided that the answer would probably be no. But she figured she could go around to the porch herself. She remembered from those July Fourth parties that it ran along the back of the house, overlooking terraced lawns and then the harbor in the distance. If she went around there on her own, too, she probably wouldn't get this servant-person in trouble.

"No, that's okay," Allie said quickly. "Here." She off-loaded the other bag. "It's heavy," she said, getting another idea when the woman reached for it. "I could take it in for you."

"Thank you."

So Allie picked up the bag and struggled with it to the kitchen, following the woman.

The hall inside the house was as she remembered it from having tea there, only darker and stuffier. It was very wide, and the walls were hung with heavy-looking land-scapes and portraits in wide gold frames. Near the door was a mahogany table holding a brass bowl of strong-smelling dried rose petals. As she followed the woman to the back of the house, Allie got a glimpse of the big parlor to the right, where they'd had tea.

The woman led Allie quickly past a wide white stair-case with a polished ebony banister that looked as if it would be good for sliding down, and through a cream-colored swinging door into the kitchen.

Allie'd never seen that room before. It was bright and

sunny, with wide counters and cupboards and a marble-topped island in the middle containing a built-in sink and stove along with lots more counter space. "Oh," she gasped, so impressed she nearly dropped the heavy bag.

"Yes," said the woman, suddenly friendlier and more human-seeming, as if she felt more at home in this part of the house. "Fancy, isn't it? But I still don't know where anything is. Our kitchen in Boston's a lot easier to get around in. I can stand in the middle and just—"

"Can Mary Scarlett have some . . ."

Allie whirled at the sound of Melanie's voice.

". . . juice," Melanie finished, staring. "Allie?"

"Hi, Melanie," Allie said, suddenly feeling shy. "Um—I brought these up for your mother." She indicated the bags.

Melanie looked inquiringly at the woman.

"She helped me carry them in, Miss Melanie. This one's mighty heavy. Wasn't that nice of her? Now," she said firmly, steering Allie to the door, "I think she'd best be on her way. You know what your . . ."

"No!" Melanie stamped her foot like someone half her age; Allie felt embarrassed. "No. She can come out on the porch with me and Mary Scarlett. Mother doesn't have to know." She seized the woman around the waist. "Oh, come on, Cookie, she needn't. And if she finds out, I'll say—I'll say . . ." She looked at Allie.

"You could say I went around to the porch myself and found you," Allie suggested quickly, trying to ignore the fact that it wouldn't really be true. "That's what I was going to do anyway," she explained to the woman Melanie had called Cookie.

Cookie shook her head. "I don't think that's a good idea," she said mildly to Allie. To Melanie she said, "Your mother's feeling kind of low today."

"Well, then she'll probably stay in her room and never know." Melanie seized Allie's hand. "Come on, Allie!" She tugged her toward the far end of the kitchen. "Oh, juice!" Melanie said, dropping Allie's hand and running to what looked like a refrigerator door without its actual body. When Melanie opened the door, Allie saw that the fridge was built into the wall.

Melanie took out a bottle of a reddish juice—cranberry, Allie decided—and while Cookie watched, shaking her head, she put the bottle and three glasses on a flowered tray, then added a matching plate and a handful of chocolate cookies from a jar on the counter. "There," she said gaily, "we'll have a party. And Mother will never, never, never know," she whispered to Cookie. "Come on, Allie!"

Still embarrassed, but also intrigued, and with a helpless shrug in Cookie's direction, Allie followed Melanie out the door.

Six

Outside was like a picture in a book of fairy tales. The porch was huge, even bigger than Allie remembered it, long and wide, with steps leading off the whole width of its front down to a lawn edged with pink rugosa roses. A few steps below that lawn was another, also edged with roses, only those were white, and below that was a third, with pink ones again. The last level down was a lawn that sloped gently to a pond Allie didn't remember, on which floated three or four handsome mallard ducks. Way beyond that was the harbor.

"I love that pond," Melanie said, butting the door shut with her rear end and putting the tray down on a round white wicker table. "Only Mother says we can't swim in it."

"It must be new," Allie said, explaining that she'd visited when old Mrs. Rochambeau was still living. Then she remembered hearing construction noises in the spring, and Ma telling her not to go up to watch lest she get in the way. "The porch looks bigger, too," Allie said. It seemed to go on and on, with little clusters of white wicker furniture here and there.

"Our parents extended the porch and had the pond built after our grandmother died," someone said, and Allie turned to see an unhappy-looking girl with a pale china-doll face and long silky blond hair lying in a chaise longue—a "lawn chaser," Ma used to call that kind of chair jokingly. Slowly the girl put down a book and got up. As her long pink sundress pulled against her front before it fell loosely around her body, Allie saw, for only a second, that her stomach was oddly rounded and poked high up under her rib cage.

"Who's your friend?" the girl asked Melanie while Allie was still staring.

"She's Allie," said Melanie. "I told you about her. Here's your juice." She handed the girl a glass off the tray. "This is Mary Scarlett, my sister," Melanie said formally. Then she giggled and added, "In case you hadn't guessed."

"I—yes, I guessed," Allie said, still staring. But there was little trace of the big stomach now, under the loose dress. "Um—hi."

"Hi," said Mary Scarlett. She lifted the juice glass slowly, with a graceful hand—on which, Allie noticed with renewed surprise, she wore a thin gold wedding band.

"Have a cookie?" Melanie said, thrusting the plate at Allie. "Cookie makes the best cookies in the whole world. That's partly why we call her Cookie. We also call her

Cookie because she cooks." She waggled the plate at Allie, nearly spilling its contents. "Take one!"

Allie did, and ate it hungrily—Ma would say rudely—in two bites.

"Have another!" Melanie said, grinning. Before Allie could answer, though, she asked, "Want to go down to the pond and feed the ducks?"

"Sure—okay," Allie said quickly, taking another cookie before Melanie put the plate down. She ate the second one more slowly, trying to savor it.

Mary Scarlett smiled wanly at both girls. "Have fun," she said languidly, going back to the chaise longue; Allie wondered if she was sick. "But don't be too long." She put down her glass and lifted her left hand, looking at a watch held by a delicate gold bracelet. "Mother should be down from her nap pretty soon, Mel. Does she know Allie's here?"

"No." Melanie opened a low white cabinet next to the kitchen door and near a shiny gas grill, fancier than the ones Allie had seen once at Sears in Bangor. "It's an adventure, isn't it, Allie?" She stood up, holding a plastic bag stuffed with bits of bread.

"I—I guess so," Allie said, feeling increasingly uncomfortable—feeling, too, that Melanie seemed sillier than she remembered. But she also seemed nervous; maybe that was it.

"When Mother gets up," said Melanie, "we'll know because the first thing she'll do is ring for Cookie. We'll hear that, and then Allie can run around to the front—just there"—Melanie darted to the right where the porch curved around the house, pulling Allie with her, and pointed out a flight of steps leading to gravel-covered level ground. "That's part of the driveway. You can just follow it to the gate, and Bill will let you out. Bill's the gardener."

"Yes," Allie said, a little dizzily. "I know. Okay. But are you sure . . ."

"Yes, I'm sure. It's so BORING here!" Melanie tugged on Allie's hand, leading her down the steps and across the fairy-tale lawns to the shore of the pond. "Mother won't let us do anything but lie around on the porch and read and play the piano. It's horrible. I hate it."

"Yeah," Allie said, feeling sorry for her in spite of the silliness. And now she didn't seem so silly anyway. "I'd hate it, too." She paused. "Maybe," she said tentatively, intrigued again, "you could come . . ."

Melanie shook her head. "She won't let us have anything to do with island people. Natives, she calls you." Melanie made a face. "Ugh! She's being so mean this summer."

Allie felt her face redden. Some of the day-tripping tourists were like that, or seemed to be, treating the islanders as if they weren't there or as if they were curiosities. Ma sometimes told about a girl she'd known when she herself was a girl, who'd jumped up and down and run around in circles, waving her arms and hooting, whenever she heard a tourist say something about "natives"; Allie felt like doing that herself now and then. But the summer people who lived on the island were like regular people—most of them, anyway. Certainly none of them had ever said their kids couldn't play with the island kids, even though it was true that most of the summer grown-ups didn't socialize much with the island grown-ups except at things like the July Fourth picnic—and even then, the two groups kept pretty much apart.

But still, they were all polite and friendly to one another most of the time.

"Anyway," Melanie said, tossing a piece of bread out onto the pond toward one of the ducks, "I'm glad you're here, and I hope you can come back." She handed Allie the bread bag.

Allie selected a piece of bread, threw it, and laughed when the male mallard dived for it. "Ducks are neat," she said. "There's a big bunch of them at my aunt's house on the mainland. Maybe someday you can . . ." She stopped, realizing Melanie probably couldn't.

"Mother has naps," Melanie said. "I think I might be able to sneak out."

"Won't you get in trouble if you get caught?"

Melanie shrugged. "I'm always in trouble," she said cheerfully. "Both of us are, Mary Scarlett and me, especially now. We're used to it."

Allie thought Mary Scarlett seemed too depressed to have the strength for being in trouble. Besides, that ring said she was married, so how could her mother still boss her around?

Why hadn't Melanie said she was married?

"Where's your sister's husband?" Allie asked casually, throwing another piece of bread out to the ducks.

For a minute Melanie stared at her. Then she said, "Oh, the ring." She glanced up at the porch and then pulled Allie over to a large white alder at the edge of the pond. "Can you keep a secret?" she whispered.

"Sure," said Allie, mystified. Why hide and whisper when they were already out of earshot of the porch?

"Mary Scarlett's not married. But she's going to have a baby, so Mother's made her wear that ring ever since she started showing. Mother doesn't let her go much of anywhere alone anyway, or me either, because she doesn't want anyone to know. She's making Mary Scarlett a prisoner," Melanie added dramatically. "It's awful. She's the one who really needs to get out, not me so much."

"But where's the baby's father?" Allie whispered since Melanie thought it was so necessary.

"That's why Mary Scarlett needs to get out. He's back in Boston. Mother doesn't like him. She doesn't think he's good enough to be in our family. And she wants Mary Scarlett to give the baby up for adoption when it's born."

"That's awful!" Allie said, horrified. "It's not her baby; your mother's, I mean!"

"Shh! That's right, it's not. But Mother's like that. She's told Mary Scarlett never to see Felipe again—that's her boyfriend. Mary Scarlett calls him when Mother's out, collect. Only Felipe's family doesn't have much money, so she can't do that very often."

Allie shuddered. She couldn't imagine a mother treating her own daughter like that. Last year when Sally French had gotten pregnant, her parents had been wicked upset, but even so they'd given her and her boyfriend a big wedding. There'd been a lot of jokes about it and some tongue-clucking, and people said Sally and Roger had made a sure-enough mistake, but no one said that they shouldn't be together or that Sally shouldn't have her baby and keep it.

"Poor Mary Scarlett," Allie said. "No wonder she looks so pale and sad!"

"I hear her crying sometimes at night," Melanie said. "Mother keeps talking about 'that baby who shouldn't be born,' and she and Mary Scarlett have big fights. I think," she said, lowering her voice still more, "that Mary Scarlett's planning to run away before the baby's born, but I don't know for sure."

"I don't blame her," said Allie. "But how's she going to be able to do that?"

"I don't know." Melanie went back to the pond and threw out another piece of bread. This time one of the female mallards caught it. "But if she is," she added, "I want to help her do it."

Seven

All the next morning, after an early driving lesson with Daddy, Allie stayed home and helped her mother wash and hull the strawberries that Ma had brought from Aunt Eulalie's farm. Then with stiff, stained fingers they loaded the berries into the Jeep, and Ma stepped back and motioned Allie into the driver's seat. Slowly, proudly, and very carefully Allie drove them both and the strawberries down to the Dockside's kitchen. She did go off the road once, making too wide a turn. But when Allie got back on it again without further mishap, Ma said, "No harm done."

"Goodness gracious," exclaimed Mrs. Trask, who owned and worked in the restaurant with her husband, coming out as Allie drove up. "Allie, is that you driving?"

Allie sat up straighter. "Yes, it is."

"How about that?" Ma stepped out of the Jeep and went around back to unload. "It's only her second day, too."

"You'd best not let the sheriff see you when he comes on here," Mrs. Trask said, winking at Ma.

"Her and half the other kids," Ma said mildly. "Katherine," she added to Mrs. Trask, lifting out a box of berries, "we're some grateful you're letting us use your ovens so late in the day. It'll be early morning from now on, I promise. But I didn't want to waste the berries Eulalie sent over and I was just too worn out last night to hull them then, even with Allie helping. Katy Porter sailed over to Eulalie's early this morning to get more; I'll hull that batch tonight."

"No trouble, Cindy, not today, anyway."

"Well, starting tomorrow, we'll be in and out before you, never fear." Ma handed the box to Allie and Allie followed her in through the restaurant's back door and into the kitchen, where freshly made sandwiches were spread out on a long table, awaiting wrapping.

"Got some tourists coming over today," Mrs. Trask remarked, stirring a kettle of simmering soup and then opening a roll of plastic wrap. "Not a big crowd yet, but I guess summer's starting."

"I guess," Ma said cheerfully, glancing around. "Now if I could just trouble you for a couple of those big bowls you so kindly offered . . ."

For the next couple of hours, after stirring sugar and flour into the berries, Ma and Allie mixed and rolled out dough, and laid rounds of it in foil pie pans Ma had brought from the mainland. Allie's crusts were lumpy at first, but she soon got the hang of it and lined her pans almost as smoothly as Ma lined hers. "I'd best do the tops, though," Ma said when they had nearly two dozen pies on the long table, long since empty of the sandwiches, which Mrs. Trask had wrapped and taken into the restaurant. Once the mailboat arrived, Allie could hear tourists stamping in and the cash register ringing as they bought sandwiches and soup and sodas and coffee for picnics on the rocks before exploring the town. "You do the filling," Ma said after stirring cinnamon into the fruit mixture. "Use this big ladle. Three ladlesful per pie, I think, will just about do it nicely."

Frowning in concentration lest she spill, Allie ladled the thick red fruit mixture into the crust-lined pans, and Ma followed her, dotting butter on the surface of the filling in each one, then settling another round of rolled-out dough on top and deftly crimping and trimming it.

"There!" Ma went down the line of pies, sprinkling cinnamon-sugar mixture on top of each. Then she wiped a wisp of hair back with a floury hand. "That's the lot. Thank goodness for the big ovens! We can get these baked and cooled by the time the tourists are ready to leave and maybe we can sell one or two. You go see how your daddy's doing setting up the shop."

Allie, glad to be out of the hot kitchen, ran next door, and found Dan tacking up a big blue-and-white sign above the newly installed screen door. CINDY'S PIE AND BREAD SHOP, it read.

"What d'you think?" Dan asked, indicating the sign.

"Ma'll love it. Pies are in the oven," Allie shouted as she burst inside to where her father was just sweeping up what seemed to be the last of the wood shavings, sawdust, and general mess from the floor.

"Perfect," Daddy said—but Allie saw him wince as he straightened up and leaned on his broom. "I bet we'll be able to open in time for the tourists when they leave on the afternoon boat. And that means we might just sell some of those pies."

"That's what Ma said. I sure hope so." She paused. "You okay?"

"Sure am, Chipmunk," Daddy said. "But you could maybe scoop this pile of sawdust and stuff up with the dustpan while I walk around a bit to get the kinks out."

Allie nodded, and after she'd cleared away Daddy's sweepings, she tried out the stool behind the main counter and peered into the green fishing-tackle cashbox beside it. A bunch of dollar bills plus a few fives and a couple of tens rested there, along with a roll of quarters, and one each of dimes, nickels, and pennies.

"Change," Daddy said, stopping at the counter as he walked by for the third or fourth time. "Think it's enough?"

"Sure!" Allie thought she'd never seen so much money all in one place.

"What we need," Dan said, coming inside and stowing his sign-hanging tools behind the counter, "is advertising. Should've thought of that."

"Yes, but where?" Daddy asked. "It's not as if we had a newspaper to advertise in."

"No," said Dan, "but what about those pamphlets they put out for tourists over to Spruce Harbor? We could advertise in those, and the mainland paper, too."

"Good idea." Daddy thumped Dan's shoulder. "Why don't you write up an ad and we'll see about sending it over?"

"I'll help," Allie said. "It'll need pictures, nice pie ones, with steam coming out."

"You're right, Allie. Maybe Miss Feathergill would do one," Dan said thoughtfully.

Allie scrambled off the stool. "I'll run up and ask her."

A few minutes later, Allie was in Miss Feathergill's sunny studio, watching Miss Feathergill, who'd agreed readily, sketch single pies, pies in pairs and groups, pies steaming, pies with a piece or two cut out. "When I get something we both like, I'll do it properly, on oaktag, so it'll reproduce well," Miss Feathergill promised, shading her latest attempt with the edge of her pencil. "Your mother's making bread, too, isn't she?"

"French bread and Irish soda bread and quick fruit breads to start," Allie answered, rattling off the list her mother had quoted to her that morning while they were washing the berries. "She says they're pretty easy, and they're kind of special, too. Later she'll make regular yeast bread if there's a call for it, but Ma says there might not be because so many people bake that anyway, on here, at least. She wants to work out how much business she gets from the island and how much from summer people and tourists before she decides what to do regularly."

Miss Feathergill nodded. "She's right to do that. Summer people'll probably want different things from what islanders want, and tourists'll be different still. That'll take some working out, I expect."

While Miss Feathergill sketched some more, Allie walked around the studio, looking at Miss Feathergill's newest paintings-in-progress—a flowery one with her garden as the model, a new view of the harbor, and a mysterious-looking ferny one in green and brown, with what looked like a tumbledown shack in the background.

"That place is right across the island," Miss Feathergill said with a nod toward the one with the shack. "I started painting it last year. It's a lovely spot, all green and mossy and quiet, not too far from where you kids make those fairy houses. Johnny Buttons showed it to me when I was wandering around over there looking for something new to paint."

"What's that shed?" Allie asked. "I've never seen it."

"An old fisherman's shack, I guess. I'm not surprised you haven't seen it. It's well hidden, kind of tucked away. But there's an inlet nearby, and I think someone must've had a weir there long ago. Might even have been my father.

He used to go away for weeks at a time sometimes, watching his weir. I was very little; he gave it up by the time I was in school, and concentrated on lobstering instead, so I don't remember much about it, and he never took me there. He might've taken my brother, but he's dead so I can't ask him about it. There's not much left of the shack. I might even paint it out, but I thought the picture needed some focal point beyond the green mystery, and I do kind of like it."

" 'Green mystery,' " said Allie. "I like that."

"Me, too. In fact, I think that's what I'll call the painting. There. How's this one?" Miss Feathergill stood up and handed Allie a sketch of two steaming pies on a table with several different-sized loaves of bread nearby.

Allie examined it critically. "Nice," she said tentatively—but she wasn't sure.

"Nice, but?" said Miss Feathergill. "But what?"

"It—well, it—there's too much in it, sort of."

Miss Feathergill peered at the sketch again. "Umm," she said. "I see what you mean. Too much separation between elements," she muttered, and went back to her table, while Allie poked around among the paint tubes and bottles of turpentine and linseed oil, and the wooden figures that she knew Miss Feathergill twisted around to remind herself of the positions in which her models sat or stood when she drew them. When Allie'd been little, Miss Feathergill had let her play with them, and with some of her colored pencils as well; when you dipped them in water, the color flowed sort of like paint.

"How's this?"

Allie looked. The breads were in a basket now, and the pies were on a tiered cake plate. "Much better."

Miss Feathergill nodded, and within the next thirty minutes she'd redrawn the sketch in black ink on stiff white oaktag and taped a flap of tracing paper over it to keep it clean. "Remember to tell your mother I want to buy pie number one!" she called after Allie.

"I'll remember," Allie shouted over her shoulder as she ran back down to the shop. When she was almost there, she saw the tourists beginning to make their way toward the dock across the fields and down from the building that housed the island's tiny museum and library. Allie, on an impulse, stationed herself at the street end of the dock, and as they passed she called out, "Fresh strawberry pies at Cindy's Pie and Bread Shop! Hot out of the oven! Take a pie home for supper! Fresh pies!"

Out of the corner of her eye she saw Daddy and Ma and Dan peer out of the shop door with startled looks on their faces, and Ma looked for a minute as if she was going to call Allie in—but then the first couple of passing tourists smiled, and when Allie pointed the way, they turned toward the shop. Ma popped back inside.

"Regular carnival barker you are," Dan said, coming up to her. "Next we know, you'll be joining the circus."

Allie thrust the oaktag at him. "Here's the drawing," she said. "Tell Ma Miss Feathergill wants pie number one. Hurry, before they're all gone!"

"No chance of that," Dan said, turning on his way in. "There's hundreds!"

But by the time the mailboat left, there were only five pies left. "One for Miss Feathergill," Ma said. "One for Uncle Ted and Aunt Hattie and Dan, one for Johnny Buttons, one for us, and one left over. I think I'll give that one to the Trasks, as a thank-you."

"The Rochambeaus," Allie said suddenly. "How about taking it to them? I could run up with it . . ."

"I don't think so," Ma said.

"Why not?"

"I just don't think so."

"But it'd be neighborly."

"Allie." Ma looked her in the eye. "Listen. Old Mrs. Rochambeau was real nice and I'd have sent her a pie in a minute. But this new Mrs. Rochambeau seems to want to keep her distance."

"Mrs., maybe," Allie said stubbornly, "but the kids are okay. Melanie and Mary Scarlett . . ." Too late, she realized she'd just about admitted to having gone inside, and from the way Ma was acting, Allie wasn't sure she'd approve.

"When did you meet them?" Ma asked severely.

"I met Melanie the other day when she was exploring. She came by when I was in the pine tree, Ma. I didn't go up to the house then. And I met Mary Scarlett yesterday when I took those bags up."

"You went inside the house?"

"You didn't say not to."

Ma sighed and glanced at Daddy, who shrugged. "No, I guess I didn't. And if you were invited in, that's all right. But Allie, I don't think young Mrs. Rochambeau really wants to associate with island people. And we don't want to make her angry, since we need the money she pays me for cleaning. If Melanie comes down to play with you, with permission, fine, or if Mrs. Rochambeau lets her invite you up there. But I don't want you going up to the white house unless you're asked. Understand?"

"Yes," Allie said glumly. "But it doesn't seem fair."

She wondered if Ma knew about Mary Scarlett—and she uneasily let Ma's words about being invited slide past without comment. Well, Cookie had invited her, and then Melanie, anyway. Just Mrs. Rochambeau hadn't.

Deep down, though, Allie knew it was Mrs. Rochambeau Ma meant, about inviting.

"No, it doesn't seem fair. Lots of things aren't, Allie. Lots of things."

Eight

"Careful getting in," Allie said a couple of afternoons later, strapping Betsy and Deirdre into bright orange life jackets. She helped them climb aboard *Starfish*, her father's old skiff—her own boat, actually, since her tenth birthday. Mrs. Corrigan had asked Allie to baby-sit while she went to the mainland for groceries, and Ma had agreed, saying she could manage in the shop, and baby-sitting was part of what Allie was supposed to do to help out anyway. Mrs. Corrigan had given Allie permission to take the children around the harbor in the skiff, to gawk at the one or two yachts that had tied up there and to watch the lobster boats coming in with the tide. Besides, Allie wanted to have a look at a big schooner that had arrived the night before and dropped anchor at the edge of the harbor, where the water was deeper. No one had recognized her, not even Daddy, who said that morning that he'd watched her come in.

"I *know* how to get in a boat," Betsy said indignantly, with all the certainty of her six years. " 'One hand for yourself and one for the ship,' " she recited grandly to her little sister, making Allie smile; she'd taught them both that, last year.

"*I* know," Deirdre replied, scrambling nimbly aboard after her and shunning Allie's offered hand. "Can I row, Allie, can I?"

"Maybe not here," Allie said. "It's kind of crowded. But you can both sit in the bow and watch for me. We've got to weave our way around all these boats and I sure don't want to hit any of them."

Betsy and Deirdre scrambled forward, nearly knocking each other over on their way and making the boat roll from side to side.

"Slow down!" Allie ordered. "One of you falls overboard, you'll scare the fish! Now sit down, both of you. No standing up, remember?"

Betsy nodded, and plunked herself down in the center of the nearest thwart, leaving scant room, Allie saw as she reached for the bow line, for Deirdre.

"Betsy," she said mildly, "you sure got fat over the winter."

Betsy looked at her, wide-eyed. "I did not!" she said indignantly.

"Then how come you're taking up a whole thwart that's big enough for two?"

Sheepishly, Betsy moved over, and Deirdre, sticking out her tongue, settled next to her, being careful, Allie saw, not to touch her.

Amused, Allie untied the bow line and pushed *Starfish* away from the dock. She'd have to keep a close eye on those two this summer, she realized. Last year they hadn't fussed at each other much at all, and Betsy had been more protective than bossy. But Allie could see Deirdre was a challenge to her now, more of a rival than someone to look out for. Sarah and Matthew aren't like that, she mused, rowing carefully past a raft of peapods and rowboats of various ages and conditions and around Clarence Fitz's skiff and the Trasks' old sloop. Maybe it's because there's three years between them instead of just one, she thought, or because one's a boy and the other's a girl.

"Allie, Allie, watch out!" Betsy called excitedly.

Allie glanced over her shoulder and saw to her chagrin that she was headed straight for Henry Phillips's mooring; she pulled to port, avoiding it—not that she'd have damaged it, but it wouldn't do to get an oar tangled in its line. "Thank you, Betsy," she said.

"Look!" said Deirdre, pointing ahead. "Look at the big blue boat!"

Allie had already spotted the fancy sailing yacht. "That's a Hinckley," she said, going as close as she dared. "See the white line on her hull?"

"What's her hull?"

"Her body, sort of. The blue part. See the line?"

"Uh-huh," Deirdre said.

"Look along it and you'll see a little loop at the end.

That's the Hinckley mark. You can always tell if a yacht's a Hinckley because of that." Allie turned the skiff and rowed alongside. "She's pretty, isn't she? You've got to be very rich to own a Hinckley. We don't get many of 'em over here, but once in a while somebody brings one over to have a look at the island. There's lots of them over on the mainland, though, over to Spruce Harbor and beyond." Allie waved at the man and the woman standing on the yacht's deck, leaning against the rail. They waved back, and then the man held up a camera and aimed it at them. A younger man was lowering a sail.

"Smile," Allie said. "Looks like we're going to be in someone's vacation album." Betsy primped and both children beamed obligingly, but Allie had to force her own smile; being photographed by strangers made her feel like a zoo animal. Still, she figured if she went somewhere special off-island, she might want to take pictures of the "natives," too.

"Thank you!" the man shouted.

"You're welcome!" Allie shouted back. That made it better. Most people didn't bother to say that.

Allie headed for deeper water and the schooner. She looked like the even bigger ones that took people cruising along the coast. Billy Clasp, the harbor master, of course would know who she belonged to, but Allie hadn't seen him to ask. She'd spent the early morning, since five o'clock, helping Ma with the pies and bread—Irish soda bread today—and the later morning taking a couple of pies in the Jeep to summer folks at the other end of the island. Daddy had made Dan go with her, but tomorrow, Daddy said, she could go by herself if there were any deliveries.

"What's THAT boat?" Deirdre asked as they approached the schooner.

"*Sea Wi-Wit-ch—Witch,*" Betsy read off the stern. "It's got *masts*! But how come it doesn't have any sails?"

"Because she's anchored," said Allie. "If they put the sails up, she might drag her anchor and sail off. She's a schooner," she added, "and my daddy said she was some pretty coming in last night with the moon on her . . ." She stopped suddenly, staring—for peering over the side was none other than Melanie Rochambeau!

"Allie!" Melanie called, waving frantically. "Allie—hi!"

"Hi yourself," Allie shouted, backing water while Betsy and Deirdre looked up at Melanie expectantly. "What're you doing there?"

"*Sea Witch* is Daddy's friend's boat. We're visiting. Come aboard?"

Allie hesitated. What would Mrs. Corrigan say? But she ached to see the *Sea Witch.*

"I—well . . ."

Melanie disappeared and returned almost immediately with a tall man who looked so much like old Mrs. Rochambeau that Allie knew right away he must be her son, Melanie's father.

"Daddy says it's okay!" Melanie shouted excitedly. "There's a ladder. And Karl will help. Are those your sisters?"

"No," said Allie, wondering who Karl was. She explained about the Corrigans, and then, before she could stew anymore about what Mrs. Corrigan would say, someone flipped a rope ladder over the *Sea Witch*'s side, and a man—Karl, Allie decided—climbed down more easily than most folks run downstairs inside a house.

The man held his arms out. "Hi, ladies," he said, bowing. "Who's first?"

Betsy and Deirdre looked at each other and then at Allie. "Is it okay, Allie?" Betsy asked.

"I guess so," Allie said. "Go on, Betsy."

"Me first, me first!" cried Deirdre, and Betsy, who seemed nervous, nodded—so Karl plucked Deirdre out of the skiff, settled her astride his hip, fastened her there with what looked like a wide belt, said, "Hang on, princess," and scurried up the ladder.

He was back for Betsy quicker than a gull dives for fish—and almost as quickly partway down again, waving one hand while holding fast with the other and saying to Allie, "Toss me the bow line, sis, and I'll make her fast."

Allie obeyed, hoping he wouldn't want to carry her up, too.

When he'd made *Starfish* fast to the *Sea Witch*, he swung his body wide of the ladder, still one-handed, and said, "Okay, sis. You look like you know your way around boats. You go on up ahead of me and I'll be right behind to catch you if you fall."

As if I would, Allie thought as she scrambled up, showing off a little.

Betsy and Deirdre were already running around the deck, jumping over coiled lines and peering around bulkheads. Melanie, in pressed shorts again—but Allie was pleased to see they were a bit rumpled this time—was standing next to the man Allie was sure was her father, watching. Allie hoped she'd seen her climb aboard.

"This is Allie Ward, Daddy," Melanie said, and the man, who looked even taller close up than he had from below, held out his hand. He had very white teeth, Allie noticed, and a pale, city-looking face. His hand was city-looking, too, but his grip was almost as firm as her own father's.

"Cindy and John Ward's older daughter, right?" said Mr. Rochambeau. "I remember seeing you once when you were a baby," he went on, "but I bet you don't remember."

"No," said Allie, adding politely, "but I remember your mother from Fourth of July, and she invited us to tea once, too, my family, I mean."

"Ah, yes. I remember those Fourth of July bashes! We'll have to do that again sometime, won't we, Mel? Gramma used to invite everyone on the island to watch the fireworks."

"Oh, let's! Could we?" Melanie asked. "It'd be easy,

Daddy, since Mother's already having that party then anyway, remember? Could we?"

"Whoops, I'd forgotten that party. I guess maybe we'd better not this summer, come to think of it. But maybe next, if we can talk your mother into coming back. We'll invite the whole island, just the way Gramma always did."

Melanie's face fell, and Allie noticed that her father's had, too. But he tousled his daughter's hair as if he was sorry, and said, "I'm sure you want to show Allie the boat. I'll just go back to talking dull old business with Mr. Harris. Okay, sweetheart?"

"Sure," Melanie said, and Mr. Rochambeau walked away.

"Is your mother really having a party on the Fourth?" Allie asked.

"A boring one," Melanie said sulkily. "Just a lot of stupid grown-ups, mostly my mother's friends from Boston. Everyone'll just stand around and drink things and talk and pretend they're not trying to outdo each other. And I'll have to wear a dress and Mary Scarlett won't even be allowed to go because of her 'condition,' which is what Mother calls it. Mother's going to make Mary Scarlett stay upstairs in her room and she's going to say she's visiting a friend. She can't even mention Mary Scarlett's baby without getting all red and flustered." Melanie paused for a moment, then continued softly. "That's why we came to Gramma's house—to hide Mary Scarlett. I'm glad we're here, but Mother hates it and she keeps saying it's Mary

Scarlett's fault that she and Daddy are missing parties in Boston and on Martha's Vineyard where all her friends go. She's having this party so her friends won't think she's 'out of circulation' and start asking awkward questions. She's told everyone that we planned to be here all along because we inherited the house, and she pretends to her friends that she loves it. Daddy really *does* love it, like I do, but he's not going to be here much." She paused again. Then she looked away, toward the island, and said, "He says it's because of business, but I think it's because he and Mother fight a lot now." Melanie's voice shook, and Allie could tell she was trying not to cry.

"There's a big celebration on the church green on the Fourth," Allie said after a moment, wanting to cheer her up. "During the day. Maybe you could come to it. There's a silly parade and games and lobsters and music—it's lots of fun. And then at night there are the fireworks. They do them out in the water, between here and the mainland, off Spruce Harbor. Like your father said, old Mrs. Rochambeau—um, your grandmother—used to have everyone up to her house—your house—and we'd sit outside and watch the fireworks and everyone would bring a supper picnic. She'd come outside, too, and go around talking to everyone. And she always wore red, white, and blue clothes and a big hat with a flag on it. But I don't guess your mother'd do that." Allie fell silent, for although Melanie had turned toward her again, her face didn't look cheered up at all; in fact, she looked downright ready to cry now.

"No," Melanie said in a small voice. "I don't think she would."

"Maybe you could come to our daytime celebration, though. Could you?"

"Maybe," Melanie said doubtfully. Then she brightened. "If Daddy's still here, maybe I could! He's always been better about letting us do things than Mother. Once in a while she gives in to him."

"That'd be great." Allie hesitated. "Would your parents really have a party next year, for everyone?"

"I would, and Daddy would and Mary Scarlett probably would, but Mother wouldn't. So I bet we won't. We might not even be here then, even if Daddy and I beg. Mother doesn't usually give in on *big* things, like Mary Scarlett's baby. She won't even listen to him about that! That's one of the things they fight about. Daddy mostly just walks away."

"I can't imagine him fighting," Allie said. "He seems so nice— Be careful!" she shouted at Deirdre, who had nearly tripped over a coiled line. "Look where you're going! I don't want to deliver you back to your mumma in a basket, for gosh sakes!"

Melanie giggled, and Allie was glad Deirdre had distracted both of them. "Those kids are so cute," Melanie said almost cheerfully.

Allie nodded. "Cute but a handful. More now than last summer."

Then neither of them said anything.

"Well, come on," Melanie said after a minute. "Karl'll watch Betsy and Deirdre." She pointed to the man who'd carried them up the ladder. "He loves kids. He's sort of the captain, I guess—the boss of Mr. Harris's crew, anyway. The *Sea Witch* belongs to him, to Mr. Harris, I mean. He's Daddy's lawyer. He's visiting, but he wants to stay on his boat, not in the house. I don't blame him. I don't think he likes my mother much."

Allie figured the only thing she could say to that was "I don't either," so she didn't say anything.

"Come on," Melanie said. "Let me show you around."

For the next twenty minutes, Melanie gave Allie a tour of the *Sea Witch*, from her bowsprit to her afterdeck. Allie was impressed that even though she was from Boston, Melanie could name all of *Sea Witch*'s masts and sails; she didn't seem a bit silly anymore.

"Now below," Melanie said, opening a door that led to a narrow companionway, which in turn led down to a tiny cabin, just big enough for an even narrower bunk with a shelf and a hammock above it. In the hammock were clothes and a book, and on the shelf were toothpaste, a hairbrush and comb, a razor, and several newspapers. It was very dark and stuffy.

"That's where Karl sleeps."

Allie shivered. "I think I'd have claustrophobia."

"Me, too. Would you really? But you're used to boats."

"Not this kind."

"Mr. and Mrs. Harris's cabin is bigger. Come on, I'll

show you. We have to stay out of the crew's quarters, though. But maybe we can have some lemonade in the galley."

Melanie led Allie aft and down a wider companionway to a cozy cabin with a tiny enameled heating stove and a pair of wider bunks. There was also a small fold-down desk and a shelf with a low fence at its edge, holding nautical and other books. "Everything opens up," Melanie said, lifting the bottom of one of the bunks to reveal storage space beneath. "When I grow up, I'm going to have a house with things built-in like they are on a boat. I'm going to get a boatbuilder to do the inside. Daddy says they're the best carpenters."

Allie nodded, thinking of the island boatbuilders. She wasn't sure they could do anything this fancy, but she'd spent a lot of time watching them, and knew her own father would trust them with just about any job—"except," he'd said once, "maybe roofing."

"Now let's ask about the lemonade."

Melanie led Allie forward again, to where Mr. Rochambeau was talking to a round man with a very red face who Melanie said was Mr. Harris, and a plump blond woman, obviously Mr. Harris's wife.

Betsy and Deirdre were nearby with Karl, who was showing them how to tie sailor's knots.

"Melanie, there you are," said Mrs. Harris, smiling. "And your friend. Allie, isn't it?"

"Yes." Allie smiled back.

"Could we have some lemonade, please?" asked Melanie.

"Of course," Mrs. Harris said. "I'll just get it."

"Oh, no, please," Melanie said. "I remember where it is. I can get it."

Mrs. Harris looked amused. "Well, okay. A lemonade party in the galley, right?"

"Right!" Melanie twirled away. "Come on," she called to the little girls. "Lemonade!"

"Karl's showing us knots," Betsy said importantly.

"That's all right," Karl said. "I'll show you more after you've had your lemonade, if there's time."

"Promise?" asked Betsy.

"Promise."

"He showed us a bowline." Deirdre skipped up to Allie and slipped her hand in hers. "It's a snake going around a tree into a hole."

Melanie laughed. "They taught us that way in Girl Scouts. I wouldn't think a sailor would do it that way. Maybe a seagull stealing fish from a boat would be better. Or a fish swimming into a net. Watch your head, Allie," she added, leading them down the companionway into the galley.

The galley was larger than Allie had expected, dominated by a longish table in the middle, with benches on either side, and a very compact stove and sink at one end. There were cupboards and bins and shelves, and a row of hooks with mugs hanging from them. Short red-and-white checked curtains covered a porthole on each side.

Looking right at home, Melanie stooped, opened a cupboard—refrigerator, really, Allie saw—under the stove, and took out a frosty plastic pitcher of lemonade. "We can use mugs." Melanie took down four and set them on the table. "I think," she said, looking at the little girls, "there are some cookies." She opened another cupboard and took out a bag of gingersnaps. "Yup. Mrs. Harris won't mind. She said this morning I could have lemonade and cookies."

"One each," Allie said firmly to Betsy and Deirdre. "Mrs. Harris might not have counted on feeding so many visitors."

"She won't mind," Melanie said again, sliding onto a bench opposite Allie. "She likes kids. Mary Scarlett and I stayed on the *Sea Witch* once for two weeks while Daddy and Mother went on a trip. Wait . . ." Melanie flipped open one of the benches and pulled out a couple of coloring books and a box of crayons. "Mrs. Harris keeps these here for visitors," she said to Betsy and Deirdre. "You can color if you want."

The children seized on the crayons and took them and the books to the far end of the table, along with their cookies and lemonade.

"How's Mary Scarlett?" Allie asked, partly out of curiosity and partly just for something to say when she saw that Betsy and Deirdre were absorbed in what they were doing.

Melanie shrugged. "Getting fatter. She says she feels like an elephant. Mostly she sits around reading or writing long letters to Felipe, which she doesn't send because she doesn't want to make him sad."

"Is Felipe nice?"

Melanie nodded. "I only met him once, but yes, he's nice. I wish Mary Scarlett would run away and marry him." She paused and lowered her voice when Betsy looked up. "And what's more, I still think she's planning to. Don't say anything, though. I'm not really sure. It's just a feeling I have."

"When's her baby supposed to come?" Allie whispered. But Betsy seemed absorbed in her coloring again.

"Around the end of August. Mother's made a reservation for her at a hospital in Bangor and she's going to take her there a week before and stay in a motel in case the baby comes early. Mother wants a social worker to take the baby away as soon as it can leave the hospital. She doesn't want Mary Scarlett to even see it. I wish I could take the baby away myself and give it to her."

"I bet Mary Scarlett wishes that, too. Or that you could get Felipe to come and take the baby."

Melanie looked thoughtful. "I wonder if that would work," she said. "I'll have to think about it."

"I'll think, too," Allie said recklessly.

Melanie held out her hand. "It's a pact, then," she said. "The save-Mary-Scarlett's-baby pact."

Allie thought the plan about Felipe sounded more than a little risky, but she slapped Melanie's hand in agreement anyway.

"Look, Allie," Betsy called from the other end of the table. She slid one of the coloring books over to her. "There's a fairy house!" She pointed to a picture of a small vine-covered cottage, with trees all around.

"It's lots bigger," Allie said, "but it does look like one, you're right. We'll have to make some more this summer, and see how the old ones are."

"Oh, yes!" Deirdre said. "Can we?"

"Sure," said Allie. "Next time I baby-sit you, okay?"

"Girls!" Mrs. Harris's head appeared in the companionway. "Mr. Rochambeau's got to be going now."

"So should we." Allie jumped up and looked at her watch, hoping she hadn't missed the tide. "Come on, Betsy and Deirdre."

"Oh, do we have to?" Deirdre said. "Karl's going to show us more knots!"

"I can show you knots," Allie said. "Come on."

"Promise about the fairy house?" asked Betsy, getting up and handing the coloring book to Melanie, who had just reached for it. "Thank you."

"You're welcome." Melanie stowed the book and the crayons back in the bench. "What's a fairy house?" she asked Allie, stepping aside to let the little girls go up the companionway ahead of her.

"A tiny house made of moss and sticks. I'll show you sometime— Oh."

"Oh, what?" Melanie asked over her shoulder as she followed Betsy and Deirdre up.

"Oh, you probably won't be able to get out."

"I got out today. And I'm going to try to get out for your Fourth of July thing."

"Yes, but today you were with your father."

Melanie turned around and looked Allie in the eye. "Don't worry," she said. "I'll get out if I want to. You'll see."

Nine

'The Fourth of July dawned clear and sharp and perfect, with a cool breeze off the harbor and the blue water a bright reflection of the sky. Allie woke up with the first warbler's song. She stretched luxuriously and lay in bed, watching the sky brighten outside her window and the pine tree's needles turn from nighttime black to daytime green as sunlight touched them. Ma had said she could lie in bed till six-thirty instead of five if she wanted, for yesterday, after Ma had come back from cleaning the Rochambeaus' house for the party, she and Allie had worked all the rest of the day baking extra pies to sell on the church green, plus several loaves of spicy quick bread using a big bunch of bananas Ma had had sent over from the fancy Spruce Harbor store that sold mostly to summer people and yachtsmen. Last night Daddy had helped wrap the bread and the pies, along with cookies and cakes and bread made by other island women. The money was all to go to fixing the church roof and maybe, if there was enough left over, to buying a composting toilet for the school to supplement the balky flush one they already had. Allie had thought that maybe her family shouldn't sell bread and pies for charity when they needed the money themselves, but Ma said, "It's in a good cause, Allie; we mustn't forget that. The money'll benefit the whole island." And Daddy said, winking, "Besides, if there's anyone around who doesn't already know how good your ma's stuff is, they'll sure find out tomorrow"—and Allie had to agree that was probably true and so would be good for business.

Will Melanie come today? Allie wondered as she finally slipped out of bed and pulled her ratty old sleeping T-shirt over her head. She hadn't seen her since the other day on the schooner, but she'd been thinking of her ever since, holed up there in that big fancy house with that horrible woman and her poor lonely expecting sister. Funny, how Melanie had seemed kind of young for twelve at first, but she'd turned out to be pretty spunky most of the time.

Allie pulled on fresh underwear and rummaged for a clean pair of shorts. She wondered if Melanie was really spunky enough to help Mary Scarlett run away to Felipe to have her baby in peace. How could she do it, though, with that witch of a mother hovering around like an osprey looking for fish?

Anyway, Allie decided, opening another drawer, it was fun having someone decent around, now that Todd and Michael had turned weird and were so full of themselves they didn't have time for her.

Allie found some shorts at last, pulled them on, and slithered into her favorite daytime T-shirt. "I'll show them today," she muttered, thinking of the softball game that was usually gotten up after the parade to kill time while the lobsters cooked. She planned to hit a few good ones and show those dumb boys she was still just as good as they were, maybe even better.

It'd be wicked fine if Melanie was there to see.

Allie passed her brush impatiently over her hair, took a last look out her window, said "Good morning" out loud to a couple of wheeling herring gulls, and bounded down the stairs to breakfast. It was going to be a good day, she was sure. The only thing lacking would be Sarah and Matthew, but Ma and Daddy said that if they came back to the island just for the celebration, they'd be homesick all over again when they went back to the farm. And they had been homesick, too; Allie'd been right about that. But Aunt Eulalie had said on the telephone the other night that they were better now, and all excited about going to the big parade they had on the mainland, and to the fireworks that night. They'd see them closer up, too, over there.

And, Allie thought, unless the weather changes—and she could tell from the direction of the wind that it probably wouldn't—it'll be a clear night, so we'll see them really well from here, too. Allie had heard that most folks were planning to go up the hill anyway, to some town-owned land next to the Rochambeaus' yard. It wouldn't be as good as the usual spot, but almost; some of the men had even cut a few trees yesterday to make a clearer view of the harbor.

Yes, indeed. It was going to be a good day.

By the time Allie, Ma, and Daddy had packed themselves and the pies and bread in the Jeep and Allie had driven them without disaster down to the church green, it was around eight-thirty and folks had already started to gather. Todd and Michael were there, obviously pretending they didn't notice or even care that she was driving. Allie hopped down from the Jeep nonchalantly and took a load of pies out with a flourish. "Morning, Todd, Michael," she said sweetly as she passed them.

"Just you wait till that ball game!" Todd called after her.

Allie turned around. "Just *you* wait!"

"Ha!" Michael retorted. "I heard that girls get real weak when they're around twelve."

Allie balanced the pies on one arm and flexed the bicep on the other; it still made a very satisfactory bulge. "You did not!" she retorted. "And anyway, you just wait and see how weak I am!"

The sun climbed higher with no clouds to tame it, and by nine o'clock, when the food was laid out on long tables in the shade of a stand of old birches, and the parade was about to start, the breeze had died down and the air was downright sultry. Johnny Buttons, ready to march and play his paper-wrapped comb, was actually wearing a cotton shirt instead of his usual flannel one, and Clarence Fitz, standing with the Wards at the edge of the island's only smoothly paved road, down which the parade would come, fanned himself with his hat and muttered, "Some hot. You'd think we was in New York City!"

"Not quite that bad, Clarence, surely," Daddy said, winking at Allie. "Don't think we could fry eggs on the road just yet."

But Allie was scanning the crowd anxiously, looking for Melanie.

Then there was the skirl of a bagpipe, the pounding of a drum, and the pebbly sound of Johnny Buttons's comb. Jamie Trask, the Dockside Restaurant's owner and the island's unofficial bagpiper—his people had come from Scotland via Nova Scotia generations ago—appeared just above the road's upper bend. Betsy and Deirdre, across from the Wards and Clarence, jumped up and down, and the harbor master's little son, Timmy, ran into the road and leaned over to one side, as if trying to see beyond Jamie and around the bend. "They're coming, they're coming!" he shouted excitedly.

"Come on back here, Timmy," said his father, hauling him out of the road. "Or you'll get squashed."

Just as Jamie Trask, in the kilt he wore only for funerals and the Fourth of July, rounded the bend, with postmistress Ginny Nichols banging the drum behind him,

Allie spotted Melanie and Mr. Rochambeau running hand in hand down the hill, and, after quickly asking her parents if she could, she ran partway up to meet them.

"You came!" she said happily, not letting the fact that Melanie was wearing a starchy-looking pink dress dampen her spirits much.

"Wouldn't miss an island Fourth for the world," said Mr. Rochambeau, handing Melanie a paper bag. "Here you go, sweetheart. There's a little house out back of the church; Allie'll show you."

Melanie reached up and gave her father a quick hug. "Shorts," she said to Allie. "Mother made me wear this dumb dress."

Allie made a face. "You change now, you'll miss the parade," she said. "Wait'll it's over."

Melanie looked at her father and he nodded. "Allie's right—it doesn't last very long, at least it never did when I was a boy. But it makes up in quality what it lacks in quantity. Look at that now!" Mr. Rochambeau pointed at the procession winding its way along the road. Behind Mr. Trask and Mrs. Nichols came an old Ford sedan carrying Mrs. Fannie Chisolm, the island's oldest resident, followed by several children on tricycles or pushing doll carriages, all trike and carriage wheels with red, white, and blue crepe-paper streamers woven into their spokes. Then came a motley crew of men and women in oilskins and bright yellow sou'wester hats, playing washboards, combs, pots and pans, and other improvised instruments. A few of them led dogs wearing red bandanas. Some of the dogs looked proud and some reluctant, but they all were panting.

"Next year," said Mr. Rochambeau, "I'm going to march with those folks if we're here. But my pie-pan playing's not up to snuff yet."

"Oh, Daddy!" giggled Melanie. Her eyes were shining now and she looked happier than Allie had ever seen her.

A couple of homemade floats followed—one a whole forest, it looked like, on an antique farm wagon, with a faded Smokey the Bear poster that read: ONLY YOU CAN PREVENT FOREST FIRES.

"Looks like the same poster they used back when I was a boy," said Mr. Rochambeau, laughing.

The other float was on a pickup truck carrying someone dressed up as a lobster and wearing a chef's hat, pretending to try to climb out of a big steaming cauldron. "Now how did they do that?" Mr. Rochambeau wondered aloud, and someone standing nearby said, "Dry ice, I believe. Welcome back, Mr. R."

"Why, thank you!" Melanie's father turned and shook the man's hand.

"We were some sorry to hear about your mother," the man said—and then both men's voices were drowned out by the siren of the volunteer fire truck bringing up the rear, with several firefighters on it, throwing hard candies to the children.

"Come on," Allie said to Melanie when the fire truck

had passed. "I'll show you where you can change. Not the little house," she added as Melanie followed her around the back of the small white church. "That's polite talk for outhouse, and it's apt to be smelly on a hot day. I think the school's open; there's a regular bathroom. You can change in there." She ran up the steps of the small two-story building behind the church.

"This is the school?" Melanie said, looking around incredulously as Allie led her inside the narrow green entryway, lined with wooden coat pegs at various heights. "But it's so tiny!"

"Well, there aren't exactly a lot of us going to it." Allie pulled a door open. "Here's the bathroom. Wait . . ." She pulled the string that was dangling from the ceiling, shedding light into the small closetlike room. Jars of poster paint were stored on a shelf above the deep old-fashioned sink, and cleaning equipment was stashed beside it, next to the miniature hot-water heater. A few rolls of toilet paper and paper towels, left over from the spring term, were on a shelf above the ancient toilet. As Allie squashed a large spider without comment and brushed away a web, she couldn't help but notice Melanie's shudder. But at least Melanie didn't scream or anything.

Still, Melanie left the door partway open while she changed. Allie found herself feeling both embarrassed and curious, so she walked away and stood near the outside door. That way she could keep anyone from coming in.

She'd seen Todd and Michael looking at Melanie with interest while the parade passed.

"Where's your room?" Melanie asked, coming out of the bathroom in light blue shorts and a blue-and-white T-shirt. Again, Allie noticed that Melanie's shirt poked out more in front than hers did. On the whole, she was just as glad hers didn't.

"My room?" Allie asked, flustered.

"You know. Your classroom."

"Oh." *Stupid*, Allie scolded herself. "It's upstairs. It's nothing much."

"Could I look at it?"

Allie shrugged. "Okay. But it's nothing." She felt embarrassed again, but differently, as Melanie followed her up the narrow staircase that led off the hall. "You probably have a great big sunny room with just one grade in it."

Melanie laughed. "It's not very big or very sunny, but it does have just one grade. Doesn't yours?"

"Nope," Allie said. "Grades five through eight. The downstairs room's for grades one through four." She opened the door at the top of the stairs, and tried to see her classroom through Melanie's eyes. The walls were painted the same green as the hall, and there were more staggered pegs near the door, higher up than the ones downstairs. Two small tables with chairs grouped around them were near the door, and about ten old-fashioned desk-arm chairs were haphazardly scattered elsewhere. An empty aquarium sat on the windowsill, along with several empty flowerpots. A set of not-very-new window-shade maps hung from the blackboard that covered much of the wall behind the teacher's desk, and an encyclopedia filled one low bookcase, textbooks another. "Real books are in the library," Allie said. "You know, stories and stuff. The library's in the same building as the town museum, down near the dock. Most of the books are pretty old, though. But look what we got last year," she added hastily. She pointed proudly to the spotless new gray computer on a table next to the teacher's desk.

"That's a nice one," Melanie said, examining it. "We've got older ones at our school. And we have to go to the media center to use them."

"Media center?"

"Library. I guess it's called the media center because it's got more than books in it."

A shout went up from outside, and Allie clapped her hand to her head. "I've got to go," she said. "Game's starting."

"What game?" Melanie asked, hurrying after her.

"Softball game. Everyone plays, kids and everyone. Hey." She turned, facing Melanie. "You could play, too!"

Melanie shook her head. "I'm no good," she said. "Really."

"You could play anyway. Everyone does. Even a few old ladies."

Melanie shook her head again, but by the time Allie had taken her down to the ball field where the teams were forming, she'd finally agreed to be on Allie's team.

"Great!" Allie said. "What's your best position?"

"Well—sometimes I pitch," Melanie said modestly.

Allie stared at her. "I thought you said you weren't very good."

"I'm not, at most things. But—" She nodded toward a couple of white-haired women who were warming up. "I think I'm as good as them, probably."

"Okay." Allie walked over to George Jenks, who was captain of the team she was always on. "This is Melanie Rochambeau," she said. "She pitches."

"Welcome to the green team, Melanie," Mr. Jenks said gravely. "We do a lot of rotating of positions. Any objections to starting in the outfield?"

Melanie shook her head. "But I can't throw very far."

"That's okay," Allie whispered. "There's plenty of people to back you up."

And there were, for the outfield was so crowded it almost looked more like the start of a race than of a ball game.

"Okay!" Clarence Fitz, who was umpire, shouted. "Green team in the field. Let's get going! Don't want those lobsters to get overcooked!"

Allie began as catcher, and Todd was first up for the blue team. "Easy out!" she shouted, but he got a double.

Then Dan was up and she shouted "Easy out!" again, kidding this time—and he got on first after hitting to right field, where, much to Allie's surprise, Melanie caught the ball after a bounce and threw it to the second baseman, which let him throw home and prevent Todd, who was just past third, from scoring.

When the green team was up and Todd was catching, he yelled "Easy out!" when Allie came up, too—and "See? What'd I tell you?" when she swung and missed the first pitch. Feeling Melanie's eyes on her, she swung at the second one, too, and missed again.

"Pull yourself together, Allie Ward," she muttered, and let the third pitch, an obvious ball, go.

The next one was beautiful; she could tell as soon as it left the pitcher's hand, and she cheered inwardly as she felt the sharp smack of bat against ball—one of the best sounds in the world, she thought, rounding the bases easily and reveling in the cheers of the spectators and the looks on Todd's and Michael's faces.

In the last inning, when the lobster cooks yelled "Ten minutes!" to the ballplayers, Melanie, who'd struck out twice and gotten a rather flabby single, finally got to pitch.

"Okay, Melanie!" Allie shouted, to encourage her—but Melanie didn't seem to hear. An amazing transformation had come over her. Her brow furrowed and her mouth tightened in concentration; she shook out her arms as if relaxing them, and took a professional stance, fixing the batter—Todd, as it happened—with a look so fierce Allie knew it would melt granite. Allie crossed her fingers and held her breath, but Melanie's father, next to Allie, with the bag containing Melanie's dress, whispered, "Don't worry. I don't know where she gets it—but . . ."

"STRIKE!" yelled the umpire—once, twice, three times—then six times—then nine times—and then, as the sportscasters say, the side was retired, leaving a final score of Green 10, Blue 8.

"Where'd you learn to do that?" Allie asked, running up to Melanie when it was over. "That was awesome!"

Melanie shrugged. "I don't know. I just do it, that's all."

"She's a natural," Mr. Rochambeau said, beaming. "An absolute natural."

Hidden talents, Allie thought that night when she was finally in bed and the island was wrapped in contented silence after the day's festivities. Melanie's got hidden talents, she thought, remembering her pitching—and, after the game, the way she'd eaten lobster, which she'd never had before. She'd tackled it like an islander as soon as Allie showed her how, even sucking meat and juice from the legs and little tail flippers. People from away almost never did that.

But there'd been a bad part of the day, too, that evening. Shortly before the fireworks started, Melanie, in her pink dress again, had run down off the porch where her parents' party guests had gathered. She came over to the hill where the islanders sat eating their picnic suppers and trying to pretend the view was as good from there as it would have been from the Rochambeaus' terraced lawns. As Melanie was settling down on the Wards' blanket to watch with them, saying that her mother was too busy with her friends to notice or care where she was, she poked Allie and pointed away from the partygoers over to the edge of the top terrace, behind the rosebushes and near the steps to the driveway. Allie craned her neck, and in the dusk she could just make out a ghostly white figure and a dark one—surely the dark one was Dan? And the ghostly one, she saw when it turned, revealing a thin but partly rounded silhouette, was obviously Mary Scarlett. They seemed to be deep in conversation. "She said she was going to sneak out of her room to see him," Melanie whispered, sounding worried. "He came yesterday, too. I think he likes her."

"He's already got a girlfriend," Allie whispered back. "I don't think it could be that. And she's got Felipe."

"Yes, but *look* at them!"

Allie had to admit it did seem suspicious. As the first rockets streaked into the sky and the crowds, both the one on the hill and the one on the porch, gasped and then cheered, Dan's head and Mary Scarlett's had bent close together—and Allie's stomach had lurched almost as if she were scared. She wasn't scared, exactly, but she knew it wouldn't be right for Dan to kiss Mary Scarlett, not when he had what Ma called "an understanding" with Katy Porter, and when Mary Scarlett was going to have Felipe's baby!

Allie tossed restlessly in bed, unable to put the memory aside.

Ten

A *week later,* Mrs. Corrigan asked Allie to baby-sit again while she went to the mainland to see a friend, and Ma, who was going to the Rochambeaus' to clean, said it would be okay but not till around lunchtime, which Mrs. Corrigan said was fine. The fog that had wrapped the island in cotton overnight lifted by noon, so Allie decided to take the Corrigan children to the middle of the island to build fairy houses and check on the blueberries, which should be formed, anyway, even if they weren't yet starting to ripen. She had nearly finished her lunchtime sandwich and led a few tourists into Cindy's Pie and Bread Shop, where Daddy was waiting for customers, when Mrs. Corrigan came in to catch the midday mailboat and to drop off her daughters.

"Can we make fairy houses today?" Deirdre asked eagerly, skipping up to Allie. "You promised we could next time you baby-sat us."

"Yup," Allie said, swallowing the last of her sandwich. "We sure can."

"And look for last year's," said Betsy.

"Oh, Allie, they'd love that," Mrs. Corrigan said. "They've been talking of nothing else. You're nice to take them." She turned to the children as the boat whistled. " 'Bye, girls. You be good now, and do what Allie says."

"Okay," Deirdre said. " 'Bye, Mommy."

" 'Bye, Mommy," Betsy echoed. Mrs. Corrigan left, and Betsy moved closer to Allie as Johnny Buttons came into the shop.

"Afternoon, Johnny," Allie said politely, handing him the sweet roll—leftover pie dough rolled around cinnamon sugar and raisins—that her mother had been making for him every day.

"Afta," said Johnny, taking the roll. He nodded at the little girls.

Allie poked Betsy. "Say good afternoon," she whispered. "He's not going to bite you."

"Good afternoon," Betsy whispered, and Johnny gave her an unsteady bow.

"Good afternoon," Deirdre said, louder than her big sister.

Johnny's mouth curled into what Allie knew was a smile, and he bowed again. This time he was even less steady, and Allie had to catch his arm to help him keep his balance. She wrinkled her nose, catching a whiff of him as he moved to the door and went out, munching his roll.

"Pew! He sure stinks," Betsy said, making a face.

"I know. He doesn't always remember to take a bath.

He has to be reminded. But you made him very happy by saying good afternoon." She smiled at them. "Ready to go?"

"Yes, yes, yes!" Deirdre shouted, jumping up and down.

Betsy ran ahead of them off the dock and partway up the hill.

"It's a long walk, Betsy," Allie said when she and Deirdre caught up to her. "Don't wear yourself out before we've begun."

"Let's sing." Betsy slowed down. "Daddy says singing helps walking."

"Sure," Allie said. "Row, row, row your boat . . ."

By the time they got to the fourth chorus, they were singing so lustily that Allie didn't hear running footsteps behind them until after they'd passed her own house. A minute later she heard another voice join theirs, so she turned around—and there was Melanie, hurrying breathlessly to meet them.

"Hi!" Allie said, surprised. "How'd you get out?"

"Mother took Mary Scarlett to the doctor. They left real early on the *Sea Witch* with Daddy. He has to go to New York."

"Allie's going to take us to the fairy houses," Betsy announced impatiently, tugging Allie's hand.

"Can I come?" Melanie asked.

"Sure!" said Allie. "Okay, girls?"

"Okay. Can we go now?" Deirdre tugged Allie's other hand.

"Yes," Allie said, laughing. "Go ahead. Who remembers the way to the woods path?"

"I do, I do!" Betsy shouted.

"Lead the way, then," said Allie, and Betsy and Deirdre galloped ahead.

"Is Mary Scarlett okay?" Allie asked as she and Melanie followed at a more dignified pace.

"Oh, sure. It's just a checkup. You have to have lots of them when you're going to have a baby."

"Yeah, I remember."

Melanie looked at her mischievously. "So when did you have a baby, Allie Ward?"

Allie felt herself blush. "Not me. My mother. When she had my brother and sister. I don't remember much with Sarah, but I do with Matthew."

"Did she throw up every morning?"

"For a while."

Melanie nodded. "Mary Scarlett did, too, at first. I think that must be the worst part. She doesn't anymore, though . . . It's so pretty here," she said after they'd walked in silence for a while.

"Yes, it is." They'd come through the first section of woods and were crossing the berry fields, a moorlike open space at the top of the island, its highest point. Straggly grass, scrub pine, and low blueberry plants grew around slabs of granite ledge, some speckled gray, some with a pinkish tinge. Here and there rainwater had collected, making tiny pools in indentations in the rocks. "We used to have picnics here," Allie said, stooping to examine the blueberries. A few were beginning to turn blue, but most were still pale green; she straightened up again.

"Used to?"

"We haven't this year. We've been too busy."

"Allie, are you poor?" Melanie asked bluntly.

"I—well, maybe a little," Allie answered, startled. "Now that Daddy can't go out in his boat. But ordinarily, no, I don't think we're poor. Maybe in comparison to your family we are, but we're the same as most island people, I guess. In good years we have plenty, and in bad years we don't. That's how lobstering is."

Melanie nodded. "It must be hard, sometimes. I wish we could give you some of our money."

That made Allie feel odd—embarrassed and angry and sad and confused all at once. She couldn't think of what to say. She didn't want to say thank you, although she guessed maybe she could for the thought. But she didn't think it would be right to take someone else's money, even if they gave it to you, when you could just as well work for it.

Melanie scuffed the toe of her shoe along a rock. "I guess I shouldn't have said that. I'm sorry."

"It's okay."

"It's just not fair for some people to have more stuff than other people."

"It's not," said Allie. "But having stuff isn't every-thing."

"No," said Melanie. "It sure isn't." She looked so sad then that Allie was glad Betsy and Deirdre came running back over the rocks, shouting, "We found the path, we found the woods path!" and that put an end to the conversation.

The woods began again just beyond where the rocky ledge sloped down, and soon they were walking past huge moss-covered boulders and among ferns taller than Betsy and Deirdre. It was cool, and so hushed and dark in the woods that they all fell silent. The little girls scanned the ground anxiously.

"There's one!" Betsy, who'd run ahead, shouted back to them. She squatted down beside the path.

Squatting also, Allie looked where Betsy was pointing, and sure enough, there was a tiny structure built of moss-covered birch bark and twigs. Just under its roof were several acorn caps. "Chairs," Betsy said, pointing them out to Melanie, her eyes shining. "We made this house last year," she said proudly. "It's the same except the chairs have moved."

"Well, of course they have," Melanie told her, glancing at Allie. "That shows the fairies used it, doesn't it?"

Deirdre nodded solemnly, and Allie was pleased that Melanie didn't need any prodding to enter into the fantasy. But Betsy looked skeptical.

"Here's another house!" Deirdre said. "Look!"

This one was larger, with two rooms and a mossy carpet. From inside came the chirp of a cricket.

"I bet he's the fairies' pet," said Melanie. "Or their horse. Maybe they ride on him."

"Let's make a bed for him," Deirdre said. "Could we, Allie?"

"Sure. Here's a nice piece of birch bark. Maybe twigs for legs?"

"Yes," said Betsy. "I'll find them. Deirdre, it'll need a blanket. A really, really soft one . . ."

The two children scurried off, hunting.

"They're great," Melanie said. "The houses. Did Betsy and Deirdre think them up all by themselves?"

Allie shook her head. "There've been fairy houses here as long as I can remember. My mother used to make them, and she said her mother did, too. And when I was real little, Ma showed me and Todd and Michael—they're the others in my class—how to make them. We didn't make them much, them being boys—it's mostly for girls. But later I showed Sarah and her friends, and last year I showed Betsy and Deirdre. This one's the best—the two-room one. I'm surprised it lasted all winter, though; it's kind of fragile . . . what was that?"

Melanie had obviously heard it too, for she was looking in the direction of the sound—a slightly muffled, rhythmic tapping. Betsy and Deirdre came running back nervously.

"What's that?" asked Betsy.

"Sounds like hammering," said Allie, frowning. She

knew there were no houses nearby, and no houses at all if you continued along the path to the shore on the other side of the island. Who'd be around there to hammer, and what would there be to hammer anyway? Chopping wood might make some sense, although there weren't many tall trees and it didn't sound like that, or like splitting logs either . . .

"Maybe someone's making something?" asked Melanie.

"If they are, they picked a funny place. There's nothing out here except gulls and crows and chipmunks . . ."

". . . and bears?" asked Betsy, her eyes round.

"And—and mooses," added Deirdre.

Allie laughed. "There aren't any bears here," she reassured them. "And the last time anyone saw a moose was when my daddy was a boy and one swam over from the mainland. I don't think we have to worry about that."

The banging stopped for a moment and then was replaced by a rhythmic whining sound.

"Sawing," said Allie promptly. "I'd say you're right, Melanie, that someone's building something—a boat on the shore, maybe—except I think I'd know about it if they were, unless it's a summer person. And why do it over here when the boatbuilder's on the other side, and tools and electricity and everything? Or maybe," she went on, her imagination working harder, "someone was wrecked on the shore—this side's bold and tricky—and they're trying to fix their boat. Come on! We'd better go see."

Eleven

There was no one, though, on
the rocky shore below them when Allie, Melanie, and the
Corrigan girls broke through the thick woods onto a steep
hill and looked down at the water. But the shore was uneven,
curving in and out, so they couldn't see all of it at once.

Allie decided that the hammering sounds—for the sawing ones had stopped—were coming from their right.

"Carefully and quietly," Allie said softly, leading the
others along the rocks and remembering the rumors of
smugglers that surfaced every now and then when people
saw unexpected lights along the shore or heard strangers'
boats late at night. "Maybe we shouldn't let whoever it is
know we're here."

"Okay," Melanie said.

They kept Betsy and Deirdre between them, for safety;
Melanie brought up the rear. Allie had already noticed that
Melanie was pretty surefooted for a city person—another
surprise, like her pitching.

The sounds got louder and clearer as they continued

walking past the place where the Wards had sometimes picnicked, although not for several years. Allie dimly remembered a narrow hidden cove beyond there—and sure enough, when they came around a stubby point, there it was. The shore was deeply indented, and the most inshore part of its curve was strewn with pebbles instead of the big boulders and slabs on which they'd been walking.

"Shh," Allie said unnecessarily, leading them along the curve of the cove. She remembered Miss Feathergill's painting, "Green Mystery," suddenly, and what Miss Feathergill had said about a hidden fisherman's shack. Maybe that was where the sound was coming from. She glanced out at the cove again; it would be a perfect place for a weir like the one Miss Feathergill had said her father might have had, maybe even one of those old-fashioned ones built of twigs and stakes, closing off the cove to trap herring.

There was no sign of a weir now, but the hammering got louder still as the little procession approached the deepest part of the indentation.

"I'm scared," Betsy whimpered.

"Me, too," said Deirdre.

"Allie," said Melanie, holding Betsy and Deirdre's hands. "Maybe we shouldn't go any farther?"

Allie shook her head. "We came all this way," she said stubbornly. "I'm sure not going to turn around now."

"I want to go home," Deirdre whined. "Maybe it's a witch."

"Listen," Allie told them sharply, "there aren't any witches."

"Are too!" said Deirdre.

"Well, there aren't any on this island, anyway," said Allie, softening a bit and looking at Melanie for help before she even realized she was doing it.

"You go," Melanie said right away, without Allie's asking, "and I'll wait here with Betsy and Deirdre. But be careful," she added as Allie turned. "Don't do anything dumb."

"I won't," Allie said. "I'll be back in a minute. In two shakes of a lamb's tail," she called back to them a few seconds later; Aunt Eulalie said that a lot and Allie liked its sound.

Melanie nodded, and Allie saw her sit down on a rock, pulling the little girls down beside her.

I bet that won't last, Allie thought, unless she knows lots of stories.

Carefully, she made her way along the rocks in the direction of the hammering, realizing only when she was halfway to the end of the cove that the sound had stopped. She paused, waiting for it to start again. But there was no sound now except the mewing of the gulls and the lapping of the tide coming in against the shore, so she worked her way back, listening and searching for a clue.

The woods bordering the rocky shore formed a thick unbroken wall, especially at the most inshore part of the indentation; there was no sign of any building on the shore itself and none of any path into the woods—but then she stopped, for dead ahead it did look as if the shrubbery parted slightly at a place between two boulders, with pebbles underneath—a dry streambed, I bet, she thought.

Allie glanced toward Melanie, who was standing now, swaying, holding hands with the children—dancing, Allie realized; she's dancing with them! Guess she ran out of stories, she thought, or didn't know any—and then she plunged into the woods, walking along the streambed— and stopped, astonished, blinking her eyes, for the woods suddenly opened into a small clearing. There was a neat woodpile near where Allie stood, and beyond it, a huge brush pile, and beyond that, a tumbledown shack with two windows without glass, screens, or shutters. A few spanking-bright new boards had been nailed over what Allie figured must be holes in the mossy weathered-gray outside walls.

Cautiously, Allie walked around the shack, but there was no sign of anyone there.

There didn't seem to be any way out of the clearing except the way she'd come in. The woods were thick and unbroken everywhere except on the shore side.

"Hello?" she said softly, then cleared her throat; no point in saying it like I don't want anyone to answer, she admonished herself. "Hello!" she called louder.

No one answered anyway.

She went around to the shack's door, stood there a minute collecting herself, and then gave it a hard shove. It swung open as if it wanted to, so, feeling a bit silly, she called, "Anyone home?" A moment later she answered herself with, "Nope, doesn't look it," and went inside.

There was just one room, and she saw right away that someone had been cleaning it, since there was a pile of sweepings in one corner—twigs and dust, and spruce and pine needles, and mouse droppings. A roll of screening stood in one corner, and two frames with glass set in them, the right size, it looked like, for the empty windows, leaned against the wall nearby. There was a rough wooden table in the middle of the floor, and a sort of shelf that Allie realized was low enough to be a bunk bed protruded from the wall opposite the glass-filled window frames. There was no mattress on the bunk shelf, but an old duffle bag, obviously stuffed full, was leaning against it.

Allie shivered, thinking again of smugglers and of an article Uncle Ted had written a year or so earlier about drug runners off the coast of Maine. They find uninhabited coves, he'd written, and put in there with their stash, leaving it for dealers to pick up.

But there's no road into here, she said to herself, so how could the dealers get the drugs?

By boat, too, of course, she answered herself, eyeing the duffle bag suspiciously. Bring the stuff here, and leave it for the dealer to come in his boat to pick up.

But why would drug dealers fix the shack up? Wouldn't that make it more suspicious?

Maybe, she thought, as she went slowly closer to the bunk and the duffle bag, they're getting ready for winter; maybe they're going to store lots of drugs here till they sell them—or maybe they're planning to live here . . .

Suddenly, Allie heard someone come into the shack behind her, and before she could turn around, whoever it was seized her arm. Allie felt a scream rise in her throat, but whoever it was let go of her arm and a familiar voice said, "Allie Ward, what in the name of all that's good and beautiful are you doing here? You scared me half to death!"—and Allie turned to look into the smudged face of Katy Porter, Dan's girlfriend.

"That's nothing to what you did to me, grabbing my arm like that!" Allie retorted in shock as well as in pain, rubbing her arm. Katy'd never been rough with anyone as far as Allie knew, certainly never with her. "I heard hammering—and I could ask you the same question, couldn't I?"

"You could," said Katy, her small pretty face looking uncharacteristically stern and maybe even a bit frightened. "But I wouldn't answer. And if you"—she seized Allie again, both arms this time, but not as roughly—"if you so much as tell anyone—ANYONE—what you've seen here I'll—oh, I don't know. Make your life miserable."

"Oh, yeah?" Allie shouted defiantly, angry as a wet cat now. "Just how will you do that, Katy? Because if you're fixing this up for some drug runners or something, I bet

Dan would want to know, and so would the coast guard and the sheriff and the selectmen and . . ."

"Drug runners!" Katy's stern expression melted into laughter and she looked like herself again. "Oh, Allie, no, it—it's nothing like that. Look," she said, leading Allie over to the bunk and sitting her down, "what's going on here is a good thing, not a bad one. It's a surprise for someone, that's all, and we—I don't want anyone to know about it because if they do, it'll spoil the surprise. Okay?"

"Who's it for?" Allie asked suspiciously.

"I don't dare tell you that either, Allie. I know you can keep a secret, but the less you know, the less of a secret you'll have to keep. Someday you'll know, though, I promise."

"When?"

"I'm not sure. When summer's over, certainly. Maybe before. Okay? Please, Allie, go away now and don't spoil things for the person this is for!"

"Does anyone else know?"

"Allie, stop questioning me! Please!"

"Does Dan know?"

"Allie . . ."

Allie shook her head. Why was Katy being so weird? It wasn't a bit like her to hide things, especially from Allie, whom she'd always treated like a younger sister. It was true Allie hadn't seen much of her lately, but even so, Allie'd thought of her as almost part of her family since she and Dan had come back after they'd both graduated from the mainland high school a year ago, with Katy wearing Dan's class ring.

Suppose Katy and Dan were in some kind of trouble? Suppose it *was* drug runners who'd put that duffle bag there, and they knew Katy and Dan knew about it?

Well, if Katy and Dan did, maybe they were planning to tell the sheriff. He'd need to sneak up on the bad guys to catch them, so of course it would have to be a secret.

But Katy *had* said it was a good thing, a surprise.

"Okay," Allie said finally, standing up and moving to the door. "I'll go. I won't ask anymore."

"And you won't come back either, right? The less you know, the less you'll have to hide."

"I s'pose," Allie said carefully, and without giving Katy time to realize she wasn't exactly promising to stay away, Allie went out into the clearing.

But then Katy called "Promise?" after her. Allie, as she headed back to the shore, decided not to answer.

"You were gone for ages," Melanie said, looking worried when Allie got back. She was showing Betsy and Deirdre how to skip stones, but Allie could see that she probably wasn't being very successful since there was a pretty good chop on the cove. "And I heard voices. Are you okay?"

"I'm fine," Allie said.

"What was there, what was there?" asked Betsy, running up to them from the water's edge.

"Nothing much, Betsy. Just an old shack."

"Can we see?"

"Nothing to see. It's just an ugly old tumbledown shack, with lots of mouse droppings and an icky smell and probably bats inside, only I didn't take the time to hunt for them."

"Yuck!" said Deirdre, who'd come up behind Betsy.

"What was the hammering?" asked Melanie.

"I don't know," Allie said uncomfortably, realizing she probably shouldn't have told about the shack. She tried to cover it by adding, "You know what, though? Miss Feathergill made a painting of the old shack last year and I bet the banging was her coming back and—and—maybe rearranging a few things. Painters do that sometimes. Maybe she wanted to change part of the painting, and she had to change the same thing in the shack so she could see how it'd look in her painting." Allie glanced sideways at Melanie to see if she believed her. Melanie looked very skeptical, but she didn't say anything—

—till much later, when they'd gotten back to the Corrigans' and Melanie was about to leave to make sure she'd be home when her mother and Mary Scarlett got there.

"You never did explain about the voices," Melanie said quietly when Betsy and Deirdre were busily drawing fairy houses at their kitchen table.

"I didn't, did I?" said Allie. "Can you keep a secret? Cross your heart?"

Solemnly, Melanie nodded.

So Allie told her everything, and made her swear again not to tell.

Twelve

The next Friday, Ma's Ro-chambeau cleaning day, the house seemed oddly quiet when Allie woke up at five o'clock. Cotton-wool fog snaked outside her window again, thick as winter snow, cutting off her view of the harbor, even of her climbing tree. Allie wasn't much surprised at first at the quiet, for fog muffles sound, but when her brain woke up more, she *was* surprised, because the quiet was inside the house as well as outside. Normally Ma would be up making breakfast by now, even on cleaning day; the house would be full of warm breakfast smells—not bacon, this summer, because of the expense, but coffee, usually, and toast to go with whatever fruit there was, or cereal. On a day like this, Allie thought, pulling on her jeans, for it was chilly, Ma'd most likely make oatmeal.

But there was no oatmeal smell either.

Rubbing her eyes, Allie used the bathroom and stumbled downstairs.

Downstairs was dark, too. The pies they'd made yesterday for Allie to deliver this morning were in their boxes on the kitchen table; they'd left the others down in the shop for Daddy to sell while Ma was at the Rochambeaus'. They'd worked unusually late last night—one of the ovens had gone on the blink and Jamie Trask hadn't had time to fix it. But Ma wasn't one to sleep in for any reason—Daddy either.

Maybe Daddy's back went bad again, Allie thought, and, alarmed, she ran up the stairs two at a time, and knocked on the door of her parents' room.

Daddy, buttoning his shirt, slid out the door, his finger on his lips. "Shh, Chipper," he whispered. "Your mumma's under the weather and we're going to let her sleep."

"But it's her cleaning day!" Allie said, alarmed again—for she knew they depended on the twenty-five dollars Mrs. Rochambeau paid on Fridays.

"She's just going to have to skip it today." Daddy put an arm around Allie and led her downstairs, where he put the kettle on to boil and reached for the tea box.

Ma almost always had coffee in the morning.

"What's wrong with her?" Allie asked.

"She says she feels as if there's a school of porpoises playing tag in her stomach. Just hand me that big mug with the birds on it, would you?"

Allie took the mug out of the cupboard. It was the one Ma put soup in for anyone who was sick. She guessed it'd be all right for tea, too.

"I think I'd better call Mrs. Rochambeau later, tell her

Mumma isn't going to make it." Daddy grinned. "Lord, looks like Mrs. Rochambeau's going to have to clean her house herself!"

Allie giggled at that idea, but she knew Mrs. Rochambeau would never do that. She'd probably make Cookie clean. Or Melanie.

Melanie.

"Daddy," she said, "how about this? How about I go do the cleaning? That way we'll still have the twenty-five dollars." And, she added silently, that way maybe I can see Melanie.

Am I a terrible person, she thought then, her face growing hot, to want to clean because of that?

Before she had time to answer her own question, her father looked at her shrewdly and said, "Would you really work if you went, instead of playing with Melanie?"

"Well," said Allie, "I might say hello to Melanie if she was even there, and we might talk awhile or something. But I'd clean, Daddy, I really would." I would, too, she thought, and I'd get us the twenty-five dollars.

Daddy took the coffee can out of the fridge and measured out enough for himself. "I dunno," he said, running water into the pot. "Get yourself some juice, Chipmunk. Maybe we should ask Mumma. We could use the twenty-five dollars, no question. Flour's running low for the shop, for one thing."

"I'll ask," Allie said eagerly.

"You'll have some juice and some toast and some milk first," Daddy said firmly, turning on the coffeepot and then pouring boiling water over a tea bag he dropped into the bird mug. "And watch this steep. I'll go up and ask your ma."

Allie poured herself glasses of juice and milk, and cut four slices of bread to toast. She could hear muffled voices from upstairs but no words. When the tea was the right golden-brown color, Daddy still hadn't come down, so she got out the tray they used when someone was sick, put the mug on it along with a pitcher of milk and the sugar bowl, a spoon, and a napkin, and took it upstairs.

Ma was sitting up, at least, but she did look pale. Allie saw a couple of new lines in her face, and her hair looked limp. Well, Allie reasoned, she didn't wash it yesterday, and she puts a kerchief on it when she cleans, and washes it after—so it's probably that and not that she's really bad sick.

"Just look at that tray," Ma said, smiling. "All pretty with the bird mug. Thank you, Allie."

"You're welcome." Allie carefully set the tray on her mother's lap. "How're you feeling?"

"Oh, it's just a little tummy upset," Ma said, adding sugar but no milk to the tea. "Mmmm—this'll fix me up fine." She took a sip. "Daddy says you want to clean for me up to Rochambeaus'."

Allie nodded. "So we can get the twenty-five dollars,"

she said. "And maybe so I could see Melanie, too," she added.

"Well, I don't know about seeing Melanie," Ma said, "although it would be fun if she could help you clean, wouldn't it? But Allie, if you go, you have to promise to really work, not spend your time playing or chatting. I don't think Mrs. Rochambeau would want you to spend cleaning time talking."

"I don't spend working time in the shop talking," Allie said, "or delivery time talking. At least not very much," she added, remembering that the other day she had chatted a bit with Coral French, who was two years younger than Allie and had just come home from Girl Scout camp.

"That's true, you don't." Ma looked at her watch. "Well, tell you what. We can't telephone Mrs. R till at least nine o'clock anyway. You go on and start your deliveries at seven as usual and come back here when you're done. If I'm still feeling poorly, we'll telephone Mrs. R."

"One change in that," Daddy said, taking Ma's hand. "Feeling poorly or not, you're to rest today. We'll call no matter how you feel, Allie and I. Then I'll go down and open the shop, and Allie'll either come down with me or go up to Rochambeaus'. And you'll stay right where you are, Cindy, no arguments."

"Gracious, John!" Ma said, her eyes twinkling. "I'm some glad I've never been sternman on your boat, the way you order folks around!"

Daddy bent down and kissed Ma, nearly upsetting the tray; Allie grabbed the bird mug just in time.

A few hours later, Allie was on her way up to Rochambeaus', on foot, because Daddy had said there'd probably be too many questions if she drove, and even though she hadn't made a steering mistake in a while, he pointed out that it sure wouldn't do if she made one in the Rochambeaus' driveway. Mrs. Rochambeau, it had turned out, wasn't at home, but Cookie said on the phone she didn't see any reason why Allie couldn't clean this once—"and," Ma said to Allie sternly, "she also said she'd keep an eye on you, so you make sure you keep your mind on dusting and vacuuming and not on gawking." She'd given Allie a passel of other directions as well, about corners that needed special attention, and about always putting things back exactly where they belonged, and about what to scrub (bathrooms) and what not to scrub (kitchen; Cookie did that).

Bill Hornby looked surprised when he let Allie in the gate. He seemed to be unusually grumpy, because of the fog, Allie thought; everyone said that always made his arthritis worse. "You again!" he grumbled. "Where's your mumma?"

"Ma's feeling sick today," Allie said as politely as she could. "So I'm here instead."

"Don't imagine Mrs. R's going to think too well of that.

You really think you can clean that house, little bit of a girl like you?" Mr. Hornby frowned down at her, holding the gate open as if he expected her to leave even though she was already beyond it.

Count to ten, Allie Ward, Allie told herself silently. *Try to feel sorry for him.* "I'm pretty strong, Mr. Hornby," she said aloud cheerfully, showing him her biceps. "See?"

Mr. Hornby said something that sounded like "Harumph!" but he closed the gate, so Allie ignored him and marched around to the kitchen door on the side of the house, as Ma had said to do. Cookie let her in, and showed her the closet where the cleaning equipment was. "Your mother starts with dusting," she said, handing Allie a large feather duster. "She does all the rooms, upstairs and down, and then she polishes the big dining-room table and the coffee table and the wooden chairs." Cookie took a bottle of furniture polish and a rag out of the closet. "And then she vacuums all the rooms. And after that she cleans the bathrooms. It's a big job, hon," she added. "Are you sure you're up to it?"

"I'm sure," Allie said stoutly, but she felt just a bit uncertain. "How many rooms?"

"Well, let's see," said Cookie. "Down here, except for the kitchen and my room, which you don't do, there's the living room, the dining room, the solarium—that's fancy for sunroom—the television room, and the library. And two bathrooms, but one's off the kitchen and I'll do that. Then upstairs there's the master bedroom, dressing room and balcony, the girls' two rooms, two guest rooms, and four bathrooms." Cookie shook her head. "Sometimes I don't know how your mother does it all in one day with no help. Seems to me you're about a third her size."

"But I'm strong," Allie said.

"And I'll help. Hi, Allie."

"Miss Melanie!" Cookie exclaimed. "Aren't you supposed to be reading?"

"I finished my book. And I'm bored. And the house is much too big for Allie to clean by herself. Besides, she doesn't know where anything is." Melanie rummaged in the closet from which Cookie had taken the cleaning supplies and emerged with another duster. "Come on, Allie," she said gaily. "Let's tackle the living room!"

In the living room, which was enormous and divided into sections by groups of furniture—"conversation islands," Melanie called them—they started acting out an elaborate story in which they were orphan sisters, doomed, Cinderella-like, to be slaves in a huge palace owned by a king and queen who did nothing all day but eat and imprison their subjects if they complained about anything. Allie got so absorbed in the story that she nearly knocked over an ugly white porcelain dog on an "occasional" table; Melanie caught it just in time.

"Oh, doom!" Melanie cried, clutching Allie. "If the queen finds out this has been moved, she'll throw us both in the deepest dungeon! I know not where it goes."

"Ah, but I do, fair sister," said Allie, replacing it.

"You have saved me once again." Melanie fell to her knees and kissed the hem of Allie's garment—her jeans, actually.

In the dining room, they planned a banquet while they worked, with roast suckling pig and quail and pheasant on the menu, "and a huge pudding," Melanie said, "in the shape of a swan, surrounded by leaves and berries." She paused, holding the duster against her cheek. "No, not a pudding; that's too soft. A swan made of spun sugar."

"For the queen's birthday," Allie supplied, "and royalty will be invited from far and wide, including . . ."

". . . including princes of noble birth, expecting to seek the princesses' hands in marriage . . ."

". . . only they don't know that the princesses are imprisoned, too," Allie said, although she wasn't really keen on the story's taking this direction.

"No, no, they don't know that the princesses are US," Melanie said, "in disguise. Only the king and queen know, but they've decided they'll live forever and they don't want their daughters taking over the kingdom, so they . . ."

"They never told them they were their daughters, never told us, I mean. But maybe," Allie went on as they moved into the solarium, which was very dark because of the fog—"maybe one of us is really a prince instead . . ."

"A foreign prince." Melanie made her duster dance across a little glass-topped table and hop over to a wicker chair next to it. "Who was exchanged at birth for the other princess, who is now locked up in a tower . . ."

"And his job," Allie said, flicking feathers over a large rubber plant, "is to free both princesses when they are of age."

"But only he knows of his role," Melanie supplied as they moved on to the TV room, "and he . . ."

She stopped abruptly, freezing in place, and Allie turned, following Melanie's horrified stare.

Mrs. Rochambeau, a look of mingled shock and anger on her face, was standing in the doorway.

Thirteen

"What is the meaning of this?" she asked Melanie, her voice agitated, with an edge hard enough to shatter glass. "Who is this girl? Where is Cindy?"

"Hello, Mother." Melanie sounded surprisingly calm, as if, Allie thought in admiration, she's the grown-up and her mother's the child. "This is Allie Ward. Mrs. Ward is sick, so Allie came to clean. I was just helping her."

Mrs. Rochambeau snatched the duster roughly out of Melanie's hands. "Making up ridiculous stories about princes and princesses is not my idea of helping," she snapped. "Go to your room, Melanie, this minute."

"But Mother, I . . ."

"Do as I say, Melanie. I'll deal with you later."

Melanie mouthed "Sorry" to Allie and went to the door. At the door, though—for her mother was facing Allie and had her back to her—Melanie turned and winked.

"Now then," said Mrs. Rochambeau to Allie, cold as fish on ice, "what have you cleaned so far?"

"The living room and dining room and the solarium and we were just finishing this room. All we've done is dusting, so far."

Mrs. Rochambeau ran her finger over a table. "You haven't done a very good job," she said, examining her finger.

"We haven't done that one yet," Allie answered truthfully.

"Don't talk back to me, young lady!" Mrs. Rochambeau rubbed her forehead as if it hurt. "Why wasn't I told of this—this arrangement?"

"My father called to ask if it would be all right," Allie explained. "But you weren't home." She stopped, not wanting to get Cookie in trouble.

"I see. So you and your father decided to go ahead anyway, without any kind of authorization."

"No, ma'am," Cookie said, coming in; Melanie must have gotten her, Allie thought. "Mr. Ward spoke to me, and I told him I thought it would be all right."

"And it's my fault," Melanie said from behind Cookie, "that we were playing. It wasn't Allie's idea; I . . ."

"Go to your room!" Mrs. Rochambeau ordered, glancing coldly at her daughter. "And you, little girl," she said to Allie, "you may leave. We'll do without cleaning today."

"What about—what about the—the money?" Allie asked.

"As you said yourself, you've hardly started." But Mrs. Rochambeau opened her purse and pulled out a single one-dollar bill. "Here. That's for the little you've done. Kindly tell your mother that I'll expect her tomorrow—her, not you. Please do not substitute for her again."

"Are you sure you don't want me to finish?" Allie asked, though she was nearly shaking with anger. "My mother might not be feeling well tomorrow either."

"If she isn't, then she should telephone me—me, not my cook—and explain. And if this kind of thing continues," Mrs. Rochambeau added, sinking into a chair, "we shall have to reconsider her position here. Now you may go. Melanie!" she shouted, for Melanie was still standing in the doorway. "How many times do I have to tell you to go to your room?"

But Melanie followed Allie and Cookie into the kitchen. "I'm sorry, Allie," Cookie said, taking Allie's duster. "Miss Melanie, you better go on upstairs like your mother said."

"I'm sorry, too," Melanie said, and she threw her arms around Allie. "Tell your mother I'm sorry." She looked anxiously at Allie. "Friends?" she said. "Can we still be friends?"

Allie was afraid that if she said anything the tears that were rising in her eyes would spill over, so she just nodded and hugged Melanie back. Then she ran out the kitchen door to the front gate, past Bill Hornby, who actually looked concerned and said, "Slow down, child, what's after you?" as he opened it—but Allie didn't answer. Her eyes blinded with tears, she ran all the way down to the dock and burst into the shop, elbowing past Johnny Buttons and nearly knocking over Billy Clasp, the harbor master, who was talking to two fog-bound lobstermen nearby.

Daddy was waiting on postmistress Ginny Nichols, who was trying to decide whether to buy a blueberry pie or the last strawberry one.

"Lordy, Allie, what's got into you?" Mrs. Nichols said as Allie hurtled through the door, and Daddy said, "What're you doing here so soon? What's happened?" He gave Mrs. Nichols a look, and Mrs. Nichols quickly decided: "I'll take the strawberry, John, time enough for blueberry later." She thrust some bills into his hands, said, "I'll get the change another time, no hurry," and bustled out.

"Now," said Daddy, "what . . ."

But at that point Allie could neither speak nor hold back her tears any longer. She buried her head against her father's chest and after a few teary minutes sobbed out the story of what had happened.

"And—and this is all she paid me, the old witch!" Allie handed him the now-crumpled dollar bill.

Daddy took it and then wiped Allie's face with his big handkerchief. "Some folks, Chipper," he said slowly, "have so many troubles that they grow a mean streak from all their worry. I kind of think Mrs. Rochambeau's that kind of person."

Allie sniffed loudly, but her nose was still stuffed; Daddy handed her the handkerchief. "She's real mean to Melanie and Mary Scarlett," Allie said after she blew her nose. "And I guess she's some mad that Mary Scarlett's going to have that baby . . ." She clapped her hand over her mouth.

"It's all right," said her father. "Your mother told me."

"How'd she know?"

"Figured it out, I guess. I doubt it was hard. Women know these things. But my Chipmunk, I do think you're right. Mrs. R's all bent out of shape over that baby she doesn't want and is trying to hide. She's so scared people will say bad things about her and her family because Mary Scarlett's not married that I guess she's driven herself near crazy with worry. I bet when it's all over with and she sees the little tyke, she'll feel different."

"She won't see it, Daddy; Melanie says Mrs. R wants to have someone take the baby away in the hospital before even Mary Scarlett or its own daddy sees it. Mary Scarlett wants to get married to him, but Mrs. Rochambeau won't let her. And I think that's wicked cruel."

Daddy nodded gravely. "I do, too, Allie. But it's not up to us to run other folks' lives. You'd better steer clear of those Rochambeaus from now on, I think."

"But Melanie . . ."

"I know," he said. "I know you like her and I know you don't have anyone much here your own age except Todd and Michael, who're feeling their boyness this summer too much to hang around a girl. There's Coral French, though; I know she's younger, but you like her."

"Not the same," Allie said, burrowing into his chest

again and feeling that maybe she wanted to stay there forever.

"Got to be, Chipper." Daddy tipped her head back and looked into her eyes. "I know it's not the same, but it's got to be."

Later that day, when Allie had helped Daddy in the shop and they'd both explained to Ma about the cleaning—and Ma, who was feeling better, had actually laughed and said, "Oh, I can just see that harpy's face when she heard you two playing over the dusting; that poor mixed-up woman's so serious she'd cry at a comedy"—when all that had happened and Allie was feeling better and more hopeful, the phone rang. Allie answered and it was Melanie asking if she was all right, and saying she was, too, except her mother had said she wasn't to see Allie again, ever.

Fourteen

Allie didn't feel like doing much of anything for the next few days. She helped Ma and Daddy in the shop, she got better and better at driving the Jeep around the island delivering pies, she picked blueberries with Coral—

"You're friends with that Rochambeau girl, aren't you?" Coral asked when they were doing that. "Isn't she stuck up?"

"No," Allie answered shortly. "Her mother is."

"I don't know, Allie," Coral said. "I saw her the other day down on the dock with her mother. And I might have been invisible for all they noticed me."

Allie changed the subject.

But the next day when she wandered up to Miss Feathergill's after working in the shop, she saw Melanie and Mary Scarlett and Mrs. Rochambeau just coming out of the studio, and it was just as Coral had said—as if she, Allie, were invisible.

She stood outside Miss Feathergill's house for a few minutes, not wanting her to see her tears. But Miss Feathergill must've seen them anyway, for she came out of the studio in her gardening clothes and put her hand on Allie's shoulder.

"Some folks," she said, "don't know what's good for them. Now I'd say that Rochambeau woman doesn't know what she's doing. Those girls are fine, but the mother . . ."

"I'm not sure about the girls either," Allie said fiercely, batting at her eyes with the back of her hand. "If you're friends with someone, you're friends, no matter what. You don't act like they aren't even there!"

Before Miss Feathergill could sit her down and reason with her, which Allie could tell she was about to do, Allie broke free from her arm and ran as fast as she could up the road to her house, and then past her house, and then across the blueberry fields and onto the high granite ledge, where she flopped down, panting and sobbing, on the warm scratchy rocks.

What's wrong with me, she thought when she'd cried herself out. I'm making a big fuss about some summer person I'll most likely never see again. And I hardly know her anyway. And I don't care, I don't care, I don't care!

But if I don't care, then why do I feel like this? Her insides were in turmoil, not quite like porpoises playing tag, as Ma had said she'd felt when she was sick, but something like that. And her head ached. And she had to pee.

Her face still stiff and salty with tears, Allie struggled to her feet, walked over to the woods at the edge of the rocks, squatted—and then looked in shock and fear and disgust and disbelief at her underpants, where she saw a small reddish-brown spot.

It wasn't as if she didn't know what it was, for Ma had explained all that to her more than a year ago. It was that she didn't want it, didn't want it any more than she wanted not to be friends with Melanie, didn't want it any more than she didn't want to go to high school on the mainland, didn't want it any more than she didn't want Todd and Michael to have turned away from her, didn't want it any more than she didn't want her family to be split up and working at the wrong things this summer.

She stuffed some old Kleenex she found in her pocket into her pants and walked back across the island, stiffly, because the Kleenex felt weird and her stomach still did, too. When she got back to the road she saw Todd and Michael throwing a ball back and forth in Todd's yard. "Lost your job?" Todd shouted.

"Lost her job 'cause she walks like a duck!" Michael said. "Look at her. Walks like a duck."

"Oh, shut up!" Allie yelled, and threw a stick at them.

"Throws like a girl now, doesn't she?" Todd said in a loud voice to Michael.

"Doesn't know she is one, though," Todd answered.

I do know, Allie thought, ignoring them as she walked on as smoothly as she could with the Kleenex bunched uncomfortably between her thighs. I know and I wish I didn't.

When she finally got back to her house she sat in the bathroom for a long time, not being quite sure what she was supposed to do next. Ma had told her what would happen, but she hadn't shown her much about what to do. But then in the cupboard she found a box of pads with stickum on the back that looked like what she'd seen in magazine ads, and she vaguely remembered Ma had said something about that, so she peeled the strip of paper off the back of one of the pads and stuck it to a clean pair of underpants and put the stained ones in the laundry hamper. Then she took them out again and put them in her closet, because she didn't want Daddy to see them and figure out what had happened.

The pad felt even worse than the Kleenex. Huge.

By the time Ma finally came home, Allie was curled on her bed because now her stomach did feel as if those porpoises were sure enough there. She heard Ma calling her from downstairs, though, so she uncurled and went to the head of the stairs and called weakly, "I'm up here." Then she went back to her room and lay down again.

When Ma came in, Allie could see she was worried, and Allie was mad at herself for not being braver, so she sat up and said, trying not to cry about it, "Ma, it's happened. You know, that—that thing you told me about."

"What's happened, honey?" Ma asked, looking puzzled,

and then she smiled, put her arms around Allie, and said, "Oh, baby, oh, baby," and rocked her as if she really were a baby.

Ma gave her some aspirin and the bird mug of milky tea and told her she'd feel better in a couple of days, probably, and Allie told her about her underpants in the closet and said, "Don't tell Daddy," and Ma hugged her tighter and said, "He'll be so proud, Allie. Please let me tell him."

"Proud?" said Allie, furious and some puzzled, too. "Why would he be proud?"

"Because," said Ma, kissing her, "he will be. You'll see."

Sure enough, later that afternoon when Allie was dozing but beginning to feel better enough to think about getting up, Daddy came into her room with a big bunch of flowers that Allie could tell came from Miss Feathergill's garden—so by now, Miss Feathergill knows, too, she figured; probably the whole island knows! But before Allie had time to be really embarrassed about that, Daddy handed her the flowers and said, "Here's for my sweet grown-up girl," and kissed her.

Allie felt herself about to cry again, and she felt mad and loving and sad all at the same time.

"You're still the same, you know," Daddy whispered into her hair.

"I'm not!" Allie shouted. "I'm not. I don't want to—be grown up, to be . . ."

Daddy smoothed back Allie's hair. "Your mumma says that lots of girls feel that way at first, Chipper. She says it's scary at first. I don't know about that. But I do know that I admire a strong, fearless woman. And that's what my Allie's growing up to be. You think about that now, Chipper. You just think about that." He kissed her again and waggled the flowers at her. "Now shall I go give these poor thirsty things some water, or shall you?"

Fifteen

Soon Allie felt like her old self again, as if maybe she could work around the changes inside her, work with them, even, or maybe ignore them. She took the skiff out a few times and challenged Todd and Michael to a race, which she won—only they said it was because there were two of them in Todd's boat and only one in hers, making hers lighter. So the next day she got Betsy and Deirdre to sit in hers, and won again. She climbed the pine tree a few times, too, and chinned herself on the branch that was just over her head, and she drove the Jeep so fast Daddy threatened to take the keys away from her. She couldn't do much about the woman part of her, she realized, but she knew she could do plenty about the strong part, so she even scoured the island's tiny library for books about muscle building and weight training. All she found was something called *The Boy's Own Handbook*, but at least that had a section on how to develop strong muscles.

"Goodness gracious, Allie, what on earth do you want this for?" asked Mrs. Porter, Katy's mother, who was town clerk for the whole island and who worked in the library two afternoons a week.

"I just do," Allie said, embarrassed and defiant at the same time—and she went down to the dock to see if there was any luggage she could help off-load.

But every time she was outside, her eyes went automatically to the big white house on the hill, and she wondered what Melanie was doing. Wondered, too, if Melanie had the same woman thing she did. Period, Ma called it, and said some people called it "the curse." "But," Ma had told her, "that's silly, because it's one of the things that lets women have babies, and that's a blessing, not a curse!"

Allie hadn't answered that, but she thought of Mary Scarlett, getting fat and lethargic and throwing up, and she wasn't at all sure Ma was right.

"Allie," Ma said one hot August morning when the heat from the Dockside Restaurant's ovens made drops of sweat roll down both their faces, "I'm going to need more berries tomorrow, and I bet we're going to have a thunderstorm later. It's too hot to breathe in here. I've got another batch of bread to do, but I can manage. Why don't you go on up to the blueberry fields and get me some more? Ought to be the last batch or so, I should think. Blackberries, soon."

"Thank goodness," Allie said, taking the blueberry-picking can—a coffee can with a string fastened to it, looped so it could hang around one's neck—and the big gathering baskets from the shelf. "At least with blackberries you get more faster."

"Ah, but there's the prickers," Ma shouted as Allie left.

That's true, Allie thought as she trudged up the hill with the can around her neck and the baskets in both hands. But she'd rather that. You could pick enough blackberries for tons of pies in half the time it took to pick blueberries.

It was even steamier in the middle of the island, up in the berry fields. Cicadas hummed and grasshoppers leapt out of the blueberry plants, startling Allie and sticking to her shorts. She'd forgotten to take a hat, and after a while, she had to go into the woods to cool off, for her face felt as if it was burning and she could see sunburn starting on her arms. It was rarely hot anywhere on the island, but when it was, this was the hottest place, for the sea breeze never got here, ever. Pretty soon she fell into an even rhythm—pick for half an hour or so, go into the woods to cool off for a few minutes, go back to picking, cool off, pick, cool, pick, cool. She felt numb with it and with the heat, kind of like a machine, and she wished she had a blueberry rake like the ones pickers used in the barrens on the mainland.

After a couple of hours, she saw the sky darken and she felt the wind pick up, and then she heard a distant rumbling. When she stood up and looked to the west, she saw a dark edge along the horizon—a sure-enough squall line if she'd ever seen one. From the way the wind was blowing, she knew the storm would be right overhead soon and would probably pass quickly. Ordinarily, Allie liked being out in the wind, leaning into it and feeling it blow her hair back. It made her feel part of it somehow, strong and clean. But a line storm like this promised to be was no joke, and from the look of the lightning flashes in the distance, she knew the last place to be, except maybe on a boat, was there on the highest part of the island where there were no trees of any size and where she was the tallest thing around.

Allie ran into the woods to get to lower ground, and then thought of the old fisherman's shack Katy'd sworn her to secrecy about. She figured, as she stowed the baskets and the can in the ferns between two boulders that formed a shallow cave, that if she ran fast she could just about get there before the storm struck.

And she did, but just barely. By the time she arrived, a cold wind was blowing against her and rain was pelting down in big drops, some of them hitting her so hard she thought they might be hailstones. Gasping for breath, she pushed the rickety old door open and fairly fell into the shack.

It was wicked dark inside, and Allie was so winded all she could do at first was sink down onto the floor and pant to get her breath back. She closed her eyes, even, for a few minutes. But then a lightning flash and a crash of thunder almost on top of each other made her open them.

She stared at what she saw, and waited impatiently for the next flash so she could see more. The shack seemed a lot cleaner and neater, and someone had made up the bunk shelf with proper sheets and blankets. A huge pot and a small one and a frying pan sat on the table, along with some chipped dishes. There were two big gallon jugs of water under one window, and a couple of cartons under the other. The windows had glass in them now, and screens.

As the storm passed overhead, easing, and daylight began to come in through the windows again, Allie got up and peered into the cartons, which turned out to be packed with canned food and an opener, instant coffee and powdered milk and cereal.

As if someone was fixing to really move in.

Allie doubted drug runners would want to do that.

Katy?

Katy and Dan!

Maybe they were going to elope?

But why would they bother? Allie knew that no one on the whole island, least of all either of their families, would object to their getting married in the regular way.

As it grew lighter inside the shack, Allie noticed a piece

of paper with writing on it lying on the table, held down on one corner by a rock:

Sweet Katy,

I think it's just about ready, but you'd best take inventory and see if we need anything else besides the stove, which I'll bring next time. What about more blankets? And maybe some first aid stuff, though I'm not sure that will really help. But we ought to have something like that, shouldn't we? Maybe you can figure out what to get?

Love,
Dan

Holy jumping mackerel!

Allie sat down on the overturned wooden crate she now noticed near the table.

Holy, holy jumping mackerel!

She wondered if she should tell anyone.

But wasn't it Dan and Katy's business if they wanted to elope?

At least that meant Dan and Katy were okay with each other, that Dan hadn't really been kissing Mary Scarlett, who he couldn't have been kissing anyway because of Felipe and the baby.

But why wouldn't he and Katy just go off in Dan's boat to the mainland if they wanted to elope?

Dan's boat . . .

The rain had stopped, and the sky was bright again; in fact, the sun was out, making the woods steam. Allie shut the shack's door carefully behind her and went down to the shore. She'd run along it so fast in the rain on her way to the shack, she knew she wouldn't have noticed a boat if one had been there. But now, looking carefully, even among the alders and sweet pepper bushes above the high-water mark, she saw no sign of one, except there was one place where the bushes were squashed down. Someone could have pulled a boat up there and hidden it, she reasoned—but why? If Dan and Katy were planning to elope by boat, why not do it from the town dock?

Well, she reasoned, because someone would be bound to see them, and eloping's supposed to be secret.

They could, she decided as she walked back to the blueberry fields, maybe have come *here* in a boat. They could have brought the cans and other stuff to the shack bit by bit in Dan's boat without anyone's suspecting. And they could be planning to go to the mainland from there with all their stuff in his boat again. It'd take two or three loads, though, probably.

She shook her head. That was much too complicated to make sense.

Maybe, she thought, stopping where she'd left her baskets and can and stooping to pick them up, shaking the rainwater through the straw of the baskets and dumping it out of the can—maybe they're planning to set up housekeeping in the shack. That'd make more sense. Trial marriage, sort of.

She'd heard of that.

Seems like a lot of trouble to go to, though, she thought, lugging the baskets across the fields and home with the can bumping against her chest. A lot of trouble.

Sixteen

Closed for Allie's Birthday!
read the banner that stretched across the door of Cindy's
Pie and Bread Shop a week later, but Allie hadn't seen it
yet. Allie's parents, plus Uncle Ted and Aunt Hattie and
Dan and Katy, were on the dock waiting when Allie came
back from fetching Miss Feathergill for no reason she
could fathom except that she'd been told to do it. She'd
been some surprised to see that Miss Feathergill seemed all
dolled up to go somewhere, wearing a flowered dress and
the big straw hat she wore only on Sundays to church, and
carrying a pie basket as if she were going on a picnic.

"What . . ." Allie began when she saw the sign and the
crowd on the dock, but before she could finish, her family
burst into a lusty rendition of "Happy Birthday," joined by
everyone else on the dock, which seemed to be half the
year-round folks on the island, plus the Corrigans and a
few regular pie-and-bread summer-people customers. Even
Johnny Buttons was there, playing "Happy Birthday" on

his comb, and when the song ended, he thrust a handful of early goldenrod at Allie, and said, "Apth day."

"Thank you," Allie said, bewildered, as Dan left the group and seemed to be untying Daddy's dinghy. "But . . ."

"We thought it would be fun to go over to Aunt Eulalie's for your birthday, honey," Ma said, beaming. "That way we can all be together and Sarah and Matthew won't have to get used to leaving the island all over again. First we thought we'd bring them over for the day, but when we talked to Aunt Eulalie about it, she suggested we all come to her instead."

"The whole island?" Allie asked, looking around, astonished.

Daddy laughed. "No, Chipper, just the family. Except"—he winked—"for Aunt Cora, who has a cold. And Katy and Miss Feathergill are coming, too. But it does look like the whole island's here, doesn't it?"

"It sure does," Allie said, turning to the birthday singers, who were beginning to disperse. "Thank you!"

"All aboard!" Dan shouted impatiently. "I think it'll take two trips, maybe three, to get out to the *Cindy One* in the dinghy. Allie, come on, you're guest of honor, so you get to go in the first load. Aunt Cindy, Uncle John, you, too."

"We're going on Daddy's lobster boat?" Allie asked in disbelief.

"We sure are," said her father. "And I'm going to take

her over to the mainland myself, too. I guess I'm better enough to do that, and pretty soon, I bet I'll be better enough to take her out hauling traps again."

"With a sternman," said Dan firmly. "Not alone."

"Yes." Daddy sighed and settled himself on a thwart beside Ma. "I know. With a sternman."

It was wonderful being aboard the *Cindy One* again. Dan had obviously shined her up for the occasion, and Allie watched her father's face as he walked around his boat, touching her gear with loving hands. She wasn't sure, but she thought she saw tears in his eyes later when everyone was aboard as he fired up the engine and maneuvered the *Cindy One* out of the harbor. She saw Ma lean against him, her arm around his waist, and then she saw her stretch up and whisper something in his ear. He leaned down and kissed her, then turned seaward again, narrowing his eyes against the sun.

Will Dan and Katy be like that someday? Allie wondered, looking at them where they sat close together in the stern, holding hands.

Maybe they do just want to get married and live in that little shack, like it's a real house. Maybe they can't afford anything else.

As the *Cindy One* purred and putted across the harbor, Allie looked back at the island, trying not to think of the day two years from now when she'd be heading for the mainland to board with Aunt Eulalie while she went to high school. That was the only bad thing about turning twelve, she thought—well, that and the other thing, the woman thing, which was still going to take a lot of getting used to. Then, as the *Cindy One* approached the end of the two armlike points that protected the island's harbor, Allie's eyes turned back to the white house on the hill and she caught herself wishing that Melanie could be going to the mainland with them.

But maybe she wouldn't even want to, the way she'd acted at Miss Feathergill's that time.

And probably she didn't know it was Allie's birthday. Ma had said she hadn't even seen Melanie again when she'd been cleaning, since that day.

As the wind stiffened, Allie turned her back on the white house and, eyes narrowed like her father's, looked ahead toward the mainland.

Aunt Eulalie and Uncle Mack's old white farmhouse sat in the middle of wide fields that had been blue with lupine in June, but now, in August, were wavy with tall grass interrupted by goldenrod, white asters, and spent lupine spikes, heavy with gray seedpods. The barn was attached to the house, set back a bit from it, though, and the chicken coop and yard were beyond that. "Nice and handy," Uncle Mack always said, " 'specially in winter when the wind comes off the water something cruel."

No one had to tell Allie or her parents about cruel winter wind, since it was crueler on the island, and crueler still out on open water, lobstering when the lobsters went deep as they did when the weather grew cold.

Now, walking in procession up to the farmhouse from Spruce Harbor's town dock, Allie felt excitement growing in her at the prospect of seeing Sarah and Matty—and sure enough, they were waiting at the edge of the road beside Aunt Eulalie and Uncle Mack's bright red mailbox. They ran out as soon as the procession rounded the last curve, and a few minutes later Allie and her parents were all tangled up in arms and legs and kisses.

"Allie, Allie!" Sarah cried, her blond braids flying, as soon as she'd unwound herself from Ma and Daddy. "We've got kittens, born just in time for your birthday, and Aunt Eulalie says we can have one. The gray one's my favorite," she added shamelessly, making Allie laugh.

"We'd better take the gray one, then. You got some tall, Sarah," Allie added, putting her arm around her little sister as they all walked up the long driveway to the house, Matthew with one hand in Daddy's and the other in Ma's. "You're near up to my shoulder already. Soon you'll be able to look me right in the eye."

Sarah giggled. "But you'll grow, too, Allie," she said. "I'll never catch up."

"Oh, I don't know," Allie said. "You might. Look how tall Daddy is, and you take after him. I take after Ma, mostly."

"And I take after EVERYONE!" Matty squealed, freeing his hands and skipping joyously ahead as they approached the wide porch. Allie saw Aunt Eulalie and Uncle Mack standing there, all dressed up as if it were Sunday, wide smiles crinkling their faces. An energetic black-and-white dog bounded up to them, tail swaying, and Allie knelt, remembering a bouncy Border Collie puppy when she'd last been there, at Thanksgiving. "Is this Spud?" she asked, nuzzling nose to nose with the dog.

"Sure is," said Uncle Mack. "He's still too unruly to work the sheep, but he's pretty good with ducks, and . . ."

"My ducks," Matthew said. "I got DUCKS, Allie!"

"You do?" Allie turned from the dog to her brother as the adults, including Dan and Katy and Miss Feathergill, went inside.

"Yes, come see, come see!" Matthew seized her hand and dragged her toward the pond beyond the chicken coop.

"They're not really his," Sarah whispered, coming with them. "But the mother duck got eaten by a fox, and Matty helped turn the eggs. Uncle Mack said he turned them so much he was surprised the babies didn't come out scrambled, with their feet growing out of their heads. But they're fine, except one died."

"He's buried here," Matthew said, pointing to a rock with "DUK" written on it in what looked like red marker.

"So I see," Allie said as seriously as she could. "Did you have a funeral?"

Matthew nodded. "Yes, and Uncle Mack read something from the Bible and Aunt Eulalie said what a good duckling he'd been and we all sang a hymn about God making all the animals and—and then we had bacon for breakfast."

"And eggs?" Allie whispered to Sarah.

"Nope," Sarah whispered back. "No eggs that day."

Allie nodded. "Out of respect," she said.

"Um-hm."

"See the ducks?" Matthew said, when they reached the pond. "One-two-three-four. They always go like that. In a line."

"They're very nice-looking ducks, Matthew," Allie said.

"Now the kittens." Sarah pulled Allie into the barn, where she knelt in an empty stall beside a large orange mamma cat with six fuzzy kittens lined up along her side, nursing. Gently, Sarah unhitched the one gray one from his mother's nipple and held him out to Allie. "Isn't he sweet? Aunt Eulalie calls him Grayling."

"He *is* sweet." Allie stroked the kitten's head with a gentle forefinger while Matthew stroked the others where they lay. "But he's much too young to leave his mother."

"Oh, not yet," Sarah said. "He can come when Matty and I go home. Or if that's too soon, we can come get him later." She put the kitten back and cocked her head, looking inquisitively up at Allie. "When can we come home?" she asked in a small voice.

"At the end of the summer, I guess," Allie answered. "Daddy's better, but today's the first day he's been out on the *Cindy One*."

"How are the pies?"

"Lots of people have been buying them. Bread, too. So I think it's helping. Daddy says we're holding our own."

"What's that mean?" Sarah asked. "Matty, be gentle! Don't pick them up." She took a squeaking kitten away from him.

"You did!" Matthew said indignantly.

"Yes, but I don't squeeze them. You do."

Grumpily, Matthew went outside.

"I think holding our own means we're making enough money to get by," Allie said, answering Sarah's question. She stood up, brushing straw off her clean shorts. "Hadn't we better go in?"

Sarah scrambled to her feet. "Yup," she said. "We're having all your favorites," she told Allie as they left the barn. "Matty and me told Aunt Eulalie what to cook."

"Thank you. Come on, Matty." Allie took his hand; he'd been throwing bits of grass to the ducks. "Now, let's see. That'd be whale stew with hermit crabs, fried rock-weed, buttered periwinkles, and, for dessert, sea-urchin pudding on lily pads. Right?"

Sarah giggled. "No," she said. "It's blueberry mush and blueberry pickles and blueberry-gravel pancakes."

"No, no," said Allie—for this was a game she and Sarah had played since Sarah was almost old enough to talk. "It's pot-warp spaghetti and toggle soup and bait-bag salad!"

By then they were at the front porch, and Sarah pulled Allie down to her level just as they were going up the steps. "Wait'll you see what Matty and I made for Daddy!" she whispered—and then they went inside.

It was a wonderful feast, and did indeed include all of Allie's favorites: roast chicken with stuffing; potatoes, sliced and fried with onions; spinach (which Matthew refused to eat); and tomato salad—with sponge cake and vanilla ice cream covered with hot homemade butterscotch sauce for dessert. "I told Aunt Eulalie to make it boil," Sarah said, "so it'd get hard on the ice cream the way you like it—and she did and it did."

"It sure did," said Allie, scraping ice cream out from under an archway of candied sauce. "It's perfect. Thank you, Sarah!"

Then there were presents, mostly practical, like new jeans and a plaid shirt and socks and a stiff jeans skirt for the first day of school. "I thought," Ma said, her eyes twinkling, "that if it was denim you might even agree to wear it." There were a couple of books from Aunt Eulalie and Uncle Mack, and a painting of the island as seen from the harbor from Miss Feathergill, and a key ring with a tiny Jeep hanging from it from Dan and Katy—and then, best of all, from Daddy and Ma, a beautiful fat Swiss Army knife with, as Dan said, "about a thousand thingamabobs on it."

While Allie was still admiring the knife, opening and shutting all its parts and trying to keep it away from Dan, who kept pretending to grab it, Sarah and Matthew left the room and came back in bearing a large and bumpily soft package wrapped in blue birthday paper and tied with green ribbon. "Colors like the ocean," Matthew said solemnly, handing it to Daddy. "Here."

"But it's not *my* birthday," Daddy protested.

"Doesn't matter," said Sarah. "Open it!"

"Seems I'd better." Daddy untied the ribbon carefully and smoothed the paper out as he peeled it off. "Well, I never!" he exclaimed, his eyes very bright, as he lifted out a large collection of newly knitted trap heads and bait bags. "Did you make these?" he asked Sarah and Matthew, who both nodded.

"They wanted so much to do something to make you feel better, John," Aunt Eulalie said, "so Mack and I showed them how to knit, and every evening just about, after supper, they sat in the kitchen quiet as little mice, knitting away."

"I never!" Daddy said again, and then he opened his arms wide. "Just you two come right here!" he said, and folded them in a huge hug. Allie could see, as Daddy looked at Ma over the tops of their heads, that the reason his eyes were so bright was because they were glistening with tears. "You are just about the best kids a lobsterman could have," he said, kissing them both. "Now I'm all set to go back to work."

"And then we can come home!" said Matthew. "Can't we, Daddy?"

"Soon's school starts, I think, don't you, Cindy?"

"I think so," Ma said.

Sarah's face fell. "But that's forever more!" she wailed.

"No, it's not," Allie said quickly. "It's only a few weeks. And besides, Sarah, you want to wait till you can bring that gray kitten home. She can, can't she, Ma?"

Ma hesitated a minute and then said, "Well, I guess having a barn cat mumma means that kitten'll know how to earn its keep."

"He comes with a year's supply of kitten food," Uncle Mack said gruffly, "if it's needed. Sarah's taken quite a liking to those cats."

"I like a good cat myself," Daddy said, hoisting Matthew onto his knee, folding Sarah into the crook of his arm, and winking at Allie. "Now did I ever tell you about Ernie, the . . ."

". . . meanest lobster east of Penobscot Bay!" Sarah and Matty chorused.

"But I forget," Sarah said craftily. "Tell us again."

"Well, along about ten, fifteen years ago," Daddy began—and as Dan and Katy slipped outside and Ma and Aunt Eulalie and Aunt Hattie went into the kitchen, and Uncle Ted lit his pipe, Allie stayed and listened along with her brother and sister and Miss Feathergill and Uncle Mack to the familiar story, "half-true and half-maybe," as Daddy called it, of a monster lobster who the men had it in for because he let other lobsters out of their traps. But one day he swam up under a lobsterman who'd gotten his foot tangled in pot warp and pulled overboard, and he carried that lobsterman on his slippery back to shore, saving both the lobsterman's life and his own, for no one ever tried to trap him again.

When the story ended and the procession headed back down to the dock to go home, Allie thought how precious they all were, her family, and how much she would miss Ma and Daddy and the kids and Dan and the island when she went to high school—but how lucky she was, if she really did have to go, to have more family to stay with, family as nice as Aunt Eulalie and Uncle Mack.

Luckier, she thought as the *Cindy One* chugged across the water in the growing twilight, than poor Melanie and Mary Scarlett, with a decent father but that horrible stick of a mother.

She still felt uneasy, though, about the way Melanie had ignored her. And she wished they'd have had time to be friends enough for Melanie to have known about her birthday.

But when they got home, there was a small manila envelope hanging from the front door, addressed to Allie. She tore it open—and inside, wrapped in white tissue paper, was a slender multicolored bracelet, woven out of narrow plastic strips. The tag on it read: "Friends forever. Happy birthday! Love, Melanie."

Seventeen

It turned out that Ma had mentioned Allie's birthday to Cookie when she'd been cleaning, and Cookie had mentioned it to Melanie, who, Cookie told Ma, had worked nonstop on making the bracelet and had begged Cookie to deliver it. And Cookie, Ma said, must have gone down to the Wards' house on her lunch break the day of Allie's birthday and left the bracelet—which Allie put on right away and didn't remove except when she took a shower—on the Wards' door.

A few days later, Daddy got off the mailboat from having a checkup on the mainland with such a happy look on his face and such a swagger in his walk that even Johnny Buttons went out of the pie shop, where he'd been sitting, to greet him.

"All I got to say," George Jenks was remarking to a group of lobstermen when Allie came out, too, "is you boys better watch out from now on." Mr. Jenks swung a couple of cartons of groceries off the mailboat and handed Miss Feathergill out onto the dock. Miss Feathergill, Allie saw, was smiling broadly, too, and she gave Daddy a poke in the ribs as she passed him. "I want the first one, John," she said mysteriously, "don't you forget. I've been waiting all summer for—for one of yours," she added after a quick look at the crowd that had gathered.

"John?" Ma said, wiping her floury hands on her apron. "What's up?"

"Doc Coolidge," Daddy said, his grin as wide as the mouth of the harbor, "says that if I'm careful, I can start going back out."

Allie watched a string of emotions chase themselves across Ma's face: first joy and relief, then worry, then the fear all lobstermen's wives live with and try to hide, then joy again—for Allie knew that Ma knew Daddy had felt like only half himself all spring and summer. She saw Ma push the worry away and force the joy to show out of her eyes as she put her arms around her husband and held him against her, partly as if she didn't ever want to let him go, and partly to show him, Allie knew, how glad she was for him.

"I've got to start real slow," Daddy said, turning to the lobstermen who'd gotten up from sitting on the dock and had circled around him, thumping his shoulders and shaking his hand, "so you boys have a little while to get yourselves up to snuff again."

"Lordy," said one of the men, "looks like John means business, boys; I'm gonna get right out there and double my string."

"You do that, Charlie, and gov'ment'll get you for sure," said another good-naturedly. "You already got the limit anyway."

"Doggone," said Charlie, "can't anyone around here keep a secret? Welcome back, John. You need any help, you just give me a holler."

"That's okay, Charlie," Daddy said. "Dan'll be working with me for a time."

"Good idea," said one of the other men. "You've got a good boy there, in Dan. Good's a son, seems to me."

"He'll be itching to have his own boat soon," said Daddy. "Long before Matthew's ready."

Allie saw her mother turn away and head back into the shop, a frown creasing her forehead. She knew that Ma secretly hoped Matthew wouldn't continue the family tradition by becoming a lobsterman—and she also knew that Ma would sooner cut out her tongue than stop him if that was what he wanted to do.

If only, Allie thought furiously, they'd let me do it!

Dr. Coolidge had said Daddy could set and haul a small string of only twenty traps the first week, and Daddy grumbled, but as Allie helped him put new heads—the ones the kids had knitted—into some of the traps that had been sitting in the yard all summer, she could see that he was eager to get started no matter what limitations he had to honor. And as she drove him and Dan to the dock with the traps just before dawn the next morning, she tried to join in his joy and swallow the ache she felt at not being allowed to go with them. "But if I take you, Chipper," Daddy had told her when she'd pleaded, "you'll just want more than ever to have your own string, and I told you that won't do. I've got to train Dan, let him have his two years' apprenticeship with me before he gets his license."

"You could train me, too," Allie had pointed out, but he'd said no then, and he said no every day after that, whenever she asked or begged.

"Listen, Allie," Ma said finally while they were rolling out pie dough in the shop, "when's the last time you heard of a woman lobsterman?"

"Never." Allie banged her rolling pin against the dough. "But that doesn't mean there could never be one, does it?"

Ma put her own rolling pin down. "Show me your arms," she said.

"Huh?"

"Show me your arms. Bend them up and tighten your muscles. Let me see."

Allie flexed them confidently. She'd been working on those muscles steadily, doing exercises from *The Boy's Own Handbook*, and she knew how strong they were.

"Hmm," her mother said, squeezing them. "You've got good muscles for a girl, and that's a fact. But when Daddy and Dan come into the shop later, you ask them to show you theirs."

So Allie did, and afterward in self-defense she said, "Yes, but I'm only twelve and Dan's eighteen and Daddy's a grown-up. It's not a fair comparison."

"You want me to go fetch Todd and Michael?" asked Dan as he left to go home.

"No, I do not!" Allie answered angrily. "But I know I can beat them arm wrestling." Allie slammed several empty pie pans into the sink, splashing herself with soapy water.

Later, when the pie pans were washed and dried and the shop was cleaned up for the night, and Allie, still sulking, was walking home with her parents, she looked at her father and said, "You told me you like strong women, Daddy."

"I do, Chipper, but there's lots of ways to be strong."

"Allie, honey," Ma said, "the fact you've got to keep in mind is that you're getting on to the age where you're developing into a woman and Todd and Michael are developing into men, and you're just plain not going to grow up as strong as them."

"It needn't be!" Allie shouted, and bolted up the road, past Miss Feathergill's and across the field behind her own house. She didn't stop running till she nearly bumped smack into Katy Porter, walking toward her across the blueberry fields at the top of the island, carrying a large empty basket Allie hardly noticed, she was so wrought up.

"Good grief, Allie, what're you doing running like that

in the wrong direction? It's nearly suppertime— Hey, Allie!" Katy gripped Allie's shoulders and held her at arm's length. "What's the matter? I do believe I see tears."

Furiously, Allie brushed her hand across her eyes. "I'm not crying!" she shouted.

"Okay, you're not," Katy said. "But something's got you mighty riled. Come on, what is it? You can trust me not to tell."

"Nothing." Allie struggled free.

Katy gave her a look. "I hear you want to go lobstering with your daddy," she said.

Allie stared at her, startled. "How do you know?"

"News travels. I guess your Daddy told Dan and Dan told me. And Dan said he had to show you his muscles."

"He shouldn't have told."

"Maybe not," said Katy, "but your Daddy was some worried about it. He knows how much you want it. Allie, listen. For one thing, I don't think the men would ever accept a lobsterwoman. For another, you're just plain not strong enough."

"Everyone says that. But I *am* strong."

"Allie, women can be strong, but I don't think they can ever be strong as men, at least not in the same way." Katy smiled. "And you know what? That really works out just fine. You'll find out someday, Allie. Want to know a secret? Sometimes I don't let on I'm as strong as I really am, so Dan'll do something for me. He likes doing that, makes him feel important. We women know we can do lots of stuff ourselves, but men like to feel they're stronger and bigger—and that's fine, too. I like feeling that way sometimes, all soft and feminine."

"Well, I don't!"

"Maybe not now." Katy reached for Allie's hand. "But you will. Now come on. It's getting late and your mumma'll worry, like you'll worry one day, Allie, when you have kids." She squeezed Allie's hand. "And listen, honey, that's something no man on earth is strong enough to do."

Two days later, Allie, still fuming, stopped up at Miss Feathergill's after her stint in the shop was over for the day. She found her putting some finishing touches on her "Green Mystery" painting.

"You seen that shack lately?" Allie asked casually, without thinking.

"No, not lately."

"Doesn't look like that anymore," Allie said, pacing restlessly around the studio. "Someone's been fixing it up. I think—" Then she realized she'd almost given away Katy's secret, so she stopped in mid-sentence and went on pacing instead.

"Well, that'd be nice," Miss Feathergill said absently. "I like it this way, though. It wouldn't be a mystery fixed up— Allie Ward, what on earth is the matter?"

"Can't women be as strong as men?" Allie blurted out. "You're a nurse; you must know. Can't they be?"

Miss Feathergill put down her brush and looked

closely at Allie. "Some women," she said carefully, "can be as strong as some men. Stronger, even. I don't think anyone really knows if women in general can be as strong. Years ago, people thought women couldn't run as far as men in races. But now we know they can. People thought women couldn't run as fast either, but that's changing, too. The fastest women can't seem to run as fast as the fastest men, but that may change, too, someday, as more women train harder. Still, since women's bodies are different from men's, maybe that won't happen even with training."

She sat down on the stool she'd been leaning against, still watching Allie closely. "Girls are as strong as boys, growing up. But around your age, Allie, most boys get stronger. A lot of that seems to be because girls and boys do different things. If a woman was brought up the way a man is, she might end up as strong. No one really knows, I think, how much is—is cultural and how much is physical." Miss Feathergill laughed. "Lordy," she said, "I sound like a textbook. Dare I ask why you're asking?"

Allie explained, but she already felt a bit better. If what Miss Feathergill said was true, maybe if she went on building up her muscles, she could be a lobsterwoman after all. She began to feel excited at the prospect, for if she could be a lobsterwoman, she could carry on Daddy's string when he got old, instead of Dan or Matthew doing it. Dan could go ahead and have his own string, and his own territory, and Matthew could do something else if he wanted— or maybe even be her sternman or Dan's.

Miss Feathergill looked thoughtful when Allie had finished explaining. "Well," she said, "I don't know how the men of this island would feel about a lobsterwoman," she said. "But you've got lobstering in your blood, Allie, and stranger things have happened. Goodness knows you're a very determined person. If any girl could do it, I bet you could!"

Eighteen

"*Letter for you,* Allie," said Ginny Nichols when Allie went to the post office for her parents the next day.

"For me?" Allie asked, surprised, taking the bundle of mail that Mrs. Nichols handed her. No one ever wrote to her.

"Right on top. Pretty, too."

The envelope was pale blue; the writing, thin darker blue lines and flourishes—fancier than her own writing, by far.

But then, Allie thought, going outside and tearing the envelope open, that's not hard. My writing's just scrawls.

"Dear Allie," it said inside in the same handwriting—gets an A for neatness, Allie thought. Then she raised her eyebrows in surprise when she saw what the rest of it said and who it was from:

Dear Allie,

Please come to my house for tea on Thursday afternoon at four o'clock.

Sincerely yours,
Letty Feathergill

"For tea!" Ma said, raising her eyebrows and looking some surprised when Allie showed her the invitation. "Miss Feathergill's? My, my, my, my! Sounds downright fancy to me, Allie. You'd better wear a dress."

Allie's heart sank. "Miss Feathergill NEVER wears dresses, Ma," she said, but when Ma looked at her cross-eyed, she blushed and said, "Well, not on here she doesn't. Not usually. Only when she's going to church or to the mainland."

"Even so, Allie," Ma said mildly, "I think you'd better. You ought to try to match that invitation, seems to me."

So on Thursday afternoon, Allie struggled into a light green dress that she hated a little less than she hated her other two dresses. She let Ma brush her flyaway hair till it shone, and she put on white socks and black dress-up shoes that had gotten too small for her. She drew the line at the straw hat with the blue ribbon that Ma handed her at the door—and she wondered, as Ma gave her a gentle push out, if Ma was somehow behind this whole scheme, what with all that talk of women not being able to run lobster boats.

But when she got to Miss Feathergill's and saw who else was there, she forgave her mother, and Miss Feathergill, and anyone else who might have had a hand in it—for Melanie ran to the door to greet her, in a yellow dress that set off her brown hair and dancing eyes.

"You came, you came!" Melanie said, hugging Allie and then leading her toward Miss Feathergill's living room. Through the open door, Allie could see that Miss Feathergill, in a wispy lavender dress Allie'd never seen before, was sitting on the sofa, sedate as the queen of England. A huge silver teapot, three fancy china cups with matching saucers, and a cream pitcher and sugar bowl that also matched were on a tray in the middle of the coffee table, along with spoons, very small dainty napkins, and a plate of brownies. They, at least, looked normal, maybe even worth putting up with the fussy tea things.

"Did you get the bracelet?" Melanie asked in a whisper, and because she was still speechless, Allie held up her arm.

"You never thanked me," Melanie said reproachfully. Then she went all the way into the room and sat down as Miss Feathergill began pouring tea.

"I—I didn't know how," Allie sputtered, going in after her. "I was afraid to call. Besides, I didn't want to get anyone in trouble by leaving messages or anything." She sat down abruptly on a stiff, straight-backed chair.

"Milk?" Miss Feathergill asked her serenely.

"Um—yes," Allie said.

"Sugar?"

Allie nodded.

"One? Two?"

"Um—two." Allie shifted uncomfortably on her chair. Her dress was scratching her, or maybe it was the chair back through the dress. "Please. Thank you."

She took the full cup and held it awkwardly on her lap, terrified of spilling it, and refused a brownie because she couldn't for the life of her see how she could balance it and the cup, too—though Melanie seemed to be doing just that with ease.

"Allie," said Miss Feathergill, when she had poured herself a cup and leaned back, sipping delicately, "I've just had two fine lobsters from your daddy. I'm so glad he's back on his boat. He must be very pleased."

"Yes," Allie said carefully, trying to match Miss Feathergill's polite conversational tone. "He sure is. So am I."

"And, Melanie, I see your father's not been able to come back since his July Fourth visit. He must miss the island, and all of you."

"That's right," Melanie answered; she sounded almost grown up, Allie noticed, as if she were used to tea-party talk. "He had to go to New York. On business."

"Ah, New York," said Miss Feathergill dreamily. "I lived there when I was in nursing school. How I longed for home that first winter! But I wouldn't have missed New York for all the tea in China." She put down her cup. "I wonder where you'll settle, Allie, when you grow up and leave."

"No place," Allie said firmly—startled, too; why bring that up? "I won't leave. Not ever."

"But there's lots of neat places, Allie," Melanie said. "Lots. Boston, where we live—I bet it's as exciting as New York."

"Oh, it is, it is," said Miss Feathergill, lifting her cup to her mouth again. "The theater, the ballet, museums. Boston has all that and more—such exciting history, for example."

"Still," Allie said bluntly, gulping the rest of her tea, "it's a city. I went to Bangor once, and I hated it."

"Just what did you hate, though?" asked Miss Feathergill. "The noise, the crowds, the shops?"

"I dunno," Allie said miserably. "I just didn't like it. Felt hemmed in, kind of."

"And that's the way we all feel right now, I expect." Decisively, Miss Feathergill put down her cup and relaxed her shoulders, which Allie could now see had been just about as stiff as that chair back Allie's own back was against. "I see we've all finished our tea, and we've certainly all been ladylike. But I can take just so much of that kind of thing. Come on into the studio—and for goodness' sake, Allie, have a brownie!"

In the studio, Miss Feathergill tied huge aprons around Allie and Melanie, gave them paper, paints, charcoal, pencils, pastels, and ink to choose from, and left them, saying she had weeding to do.

"Hi," said Melanie as soon as Miss Feathergill had gone.

"Hi," Allie answered, still mystified.

"The tea party was a put-up job," Melanie told her, selecting a large sheet of paper. "I got the idea when Mary Scarlett and Mother and I had tea with Miss Feathergill before—that awful day when I didn't dare speak to you? It was a really fancy tea like today, only it went on and on and on. But then I thought Mother might let me have tea with Miss Feathergill alone; Mother approves of her because of Miss Feathergill being an artist. Miss Feathergill even has two paintings in a gallery in Boston my mother goes to a lot. Mother said it would be all right and that it might make me less of a savage, and then I asked Miss Feathergill to invite you. So Miss Feathergill asked your mother and she said yes . . ."

"Your mother, Allie," said Miss Feathergill, coming back into the room with the brownies, "said she didn't think it would hurt for you to have a formal tea party. Hence the charade in the living room. Enjoy—I don't want there to be any leftovers," she said, leaving again. "Come out to the garden if you get bored here."

Allie, still somewhat bewildered, took a brownie at last.

Melanie opened a box of watercolors. "Anyway," she said with satisfaction, "it worked, because here you are."

"Here I am," said Allie, scratching vigorously. The back of her neck itched like crazy, right where the dress's label was.

"I think Mother's going to take Mary Scarlett to Bangor in a week or two. She's getting really fat."

"I wish we could help her," Allie said cautiously. "It's so awful about her baby."

"Mary Scarlett won't even talk about it, but I still hear her crying a lot. I think women get weird when they're pregnant. It's kind of interesting, but kind of annoying, too. I'm really sorry for her, but I wish she could be—well, stronger, I guess. If I were her, I'd have run away ages ago, but Mary Scarlett's not like that." Melanie picked up a pencil and started sketching. "She's always been good. She always did what Mother wanted till she started seeing Felipe. I think that's why Mother's been so upset. And Mother keeps calling Felipe 'that foreign boy,' but he's not all that foreign, only Puerto Rican, and he's really, really nice."

Melanie paused for a moment as if waiting for a re-action, but Allie couldn't think of anything to say, even though she wanted to say something. But everything she thought of sounded dumb.

"I really liked those fairy houses you showed me," Melanie finally said. "I wish I could see them again."

"I wish you could, too," Allie replied eagerly; at least she could talk about that. "Hey, I know! Maybe we could go now. Miss Feathergill wouldn't mind, I bet. And you're here and all . . ."

Melanie shook her head. "We're bound to get dirty.

Mother'll kill me if I do. And then she'll figure out I wasn't here the whole time, and that'll get Miss Feathergill in trouble."

"Well, then," Allie said as the idea hit her. "I'll draw you a fairy house."

"Okay! And I'll draw you—I'll draw you my room here in Gramma's house. My island room. I was going to show it to you when you were there, cleaning, but then we got caught . . ."

For a while, they worked quietly except for Allie telling Melanie about seeing the fisherman's shack again, and Melanie telling Allie that she hadn't been able to find out anything concrete about Mary Scarlett's plans. "But I've heard her twice lately whispering on the phone. It must have been to Felipe."

"Yeah," said Allie. "I bet it was."

Then they both fell silent.

Allie used up seven pieces of paper before she finally finished a drawing she thought would do. Melanie, she noticed, stuck to one piece, but she did a lot of erasing of pencil lines before she painted. Allie decided not to paint hers, except at the top, where she painted "For Melanie" in green, and at the bottom, smaller, but also in green, where she painted "Friends Forever, Allie."

"I love it," Melanie said, looking over Allie's shoulder. "Here's mine." She showed Allie her picture. It was a little lopsided, but very clear—a bed, with a small white table beside it, a white bureau, a white dressing table with a skirt, and white curtains, all against pale yellow walls with blue dots. "They're really flowers," Melanie said, pointing to them, "but they're so tiny they look like dots unless you're right on top of them."

"It's pretty," said Allie, thinking that it looked perfect for Melanie. But she figured you couldn't walk into a room like that if you'd been out lobstering, or even picking berries or baking the way she and Ma baked.

"What's your room like?"

"Oh, it's kind of simple," Allie said nonchalantly. "Plain. It's got a neat window, though, with that big old pine tree right outside that I was climbing when you first came. I can see it from my bed. What's your room in Boston like?"

"It's smaller than the one here," Melanie told her. "And it has light blue walls. There are lots of books. And my old dolls and stuff are all over the place. It's kind of a mess, really."

"I only ever had one doll," said Allie. "His name was Michael. But I had a bunch of stuffed animals."

"I had the neatest stuffed cat," said Melanie. "Fluffy. I used to take her to school and dress her up and everything."

"I took my animals out in my father's skiff once," Allie said. "You know, for a ride. One of them fell overboard and I had to fish her out. I almost fell overboard myself. Ma hung her up to dry on the clothesline by her ears. I thought that must've hurt some bad."

Melanie laughed, and at the same time put her hand on Allie's arm. "It must've," she said. "Mother had Cookie wash Fluffy once, and put her in the dryer."

"Ouch!" said Allie.

"Yes, ouch. I cried. But at least she was fluffy again when she came out."

Miss Feathergill appeared in the doorway, wearing her gardening clothes. "Ladies," she said, "I'm afraid it's five-thirty. Allie, you'd better get back home or your mother'll wonder what's keeping you. And Melanie, I think I see that fire engine of your mother's coming down the hill . . ."

"Quick, Allie," Melanie cried in alarm, "you'd better run!"

"Run?" said Miss Feathergill. "Why on earth? In that dress and those shoes? Impossible!"

In a flash, Allie realized that Miss Feathergill didn't know that Melanie wasn't supposed to see her. "I'll stay inside, Melanie," she said quickly, "and you go out to meet your mother before she comes in. Go on, quick. Thank you for the picture," she added.

"Thank you for yours. Remember," Melanie whispered right before she dashed out the door. "Friends forever!"

"Yes." Allie felt a warm glow spread over her and wondered how she could ever have thought Melanie was silly or stuck up. "Friends forever! Go, hurry!"

"Allie," said Miss Feathergill, when she'd waved at Mrs. Rochambeau as Melanie got into the fire-engine-red car, "is there something going on here I should know about?"

"Um, well, maybe." Allie watched the car make its way up the hill. "But it might be safer if you didn't know. Thanks for the tea and the brownies," she said before Miss Feathergill had time to question her further. And as soon as Mrs. Rochambeau's car was out of sight, she dashed out the door and home to supper.

Nineteen

"*I don't think* it'll hit us straight on," Daddy said a few afternoons later, squinting up at a yellowish sky when he and Dan came wearily into the pie shop. "But we're going to have a heck of a blow, no question. There's a good chop out on the harbor already."

Ma poured a mug of coffee for him and one for Dan. The morning had been hot and muggy, close and still, a real weather breeder, the men all said, and the radio said there were hurricane warnings up along the coast to the south.

"A big blow here for sure," Dan said, swallowing coffee gratefully. "Thanks, Aunt Cindy. It's some cold out there now in that wind. And the *Cindy One* was pitching like she thought she was a bucking bronco in the Old West."

"George says he's not sure about taking the mailboat on the afternoon run," Daddy said. "And I'm all in." He stood, stretching, and put one hand against his back.

"You have Allie run you up to the house in the Jeep, John, and no arguing." Ma handed Allie the keys and gave her a shove. "And you lie down, flat, and don't move till I get home. See he does it, Allie. You go on, too, Dan. You might's well ride along in the Jeep yourself. You look pretty tuckered out."

"No, I guess I'll go on up to Katy's," Dan said casually. "See if her folks need anything."

"Well, have Allie drop you off, then."

"Good idea," Dan said. "Okay, Allie?"

"Sure," Allie answered, eager to be out in the wind for as long as Daddy and Ma would let her stay. They'd worry about branches and wires falling, she knew, once the storm got going. But although it looked as if there was going to be a lot of rain, there was no sign of lightning yet, and if that held off, she might be allowed to stay outside feeling the wind till the storm really hit.

Walking was already hard when Allie and Daddy and Dan left the shop. Allie had to give the Jeep more gas than usual to get it up the hill to drop Daddy off, and then even more gas to continue on to Katy's.

As she was turning the Jeep around in Katy's driveway right after Dan got out, Allie saw Katy burst out of her house and run to Dan, stopping him before he'd gotten even halfway to the door, and waving her arms around as if she was wicked rattled about something. Allie saw Dan nod, give Katy a quick hug, and head back down the hill, running as fast as she reckoned he could with the wind blowing crosswise like it was.

"Wonder what that's all about," she muttered as she

drove the short distance home, parked the Jeep, and went inside.

"You lying down, Daddy?" Allie called. She could hear the crackle of his shortwave radio from upstairs.

"I am indeed," her father called down to her. "But you better go down to the shop and get your ma. George has canceled the mailboat and there's gale warnings all the way into Canada. This one's no joke, Allie."

"Okay."

Rain had started, so Allie pulled her yellow slicker on—no time, she figured, for the oilskin pants—and started up the Jeep again.

Her mother was helping the Trasks hammer plywood over the Dockside's windows and the shop's, too—just in case, they all said, it turned out to be more than only a wicked big blow.

"Go on, Cindy," Jamie Trask shouted when Allie honked the Jeep's horn. "Get on home. We'll finish up here. Go on, woman, 'fore you get blown away."

Ma waved and climbed in beside Allie. Allie could see men securing loose gear on the docks, and one or two were still rowing in from their boats, moored out in the harbor.

"It's not really raining that hard yet," Ma said, "but my goodness, that wind sure makes the drops sting! Your father all right?"

"He said he was lying down," Allie said, turning the Jeep, "but I could hear the shortwave so I'm not sure."

"Men!" said her mother. "Got to have his nose in

everything, your father. Well, at least he's off the water, and that's some comfort. Watch out!" she shouted as a tree limb snapped off dangerously close to the Jeep.

Allie swerved in time to avoid it, and a few minutes later pulled the Jeep safely into the driveway.

For the next few hours, Ma and Allie huddled by a kerosene lamp next to where Daddy lay in bed, for the electricity went out just about when they got home. Later, they all ate soup warmed up on the camp stove, and kept track of the storm on the battery radio. Farther south, it said, the winds were at hurricane force; there was bad coastal flooding and the storm had stalled, but the worst of it wasn't expected to come any farther north.

"Might as well go to sleep," Daddy said eventually. "Let this thing blow itself out. Seems quieter now, anyway."

And it did. By the time Allie had put on her sleeping T-shirt and crawled into bed, the howling outside had abated, and she fell asleep quickly, lulled by the more softly blowing wind.

But a while later—she had no idea how much later—she woke to an odd rhythmical noise, as if a branch were tapping against her window over and over again. The storm's started up again, she thought, snuggling deeper into her pillow. But the sound continued, and finally, reluctantly, she opened her eyes.

A yellow light was playing against her window, like a spotlight or a flashlight. That's it, flashlight, she thought, alarmed, as she got up and opened the window. Sure enough, someone was down there on the ground, shining a light up at her. "Allie," a voice called hoarsely, half a shout and half a whisper. "Allie, oh, Allie, please get up!"

"Melanie?" Allie said, blinking, trying to focus her eyes—for it did sound like Melanie, and the figure below on the ground was small enough.

"Yes, it's me. Allie, Mary Scarlett's missing and I have an idea where she's gone. Hurry, please. Can you come help?"

Allie snapped instantly awake. "I'll be right there," she said, and pulled on her clothes. Then, taking a flashlight from the table beside her bed, she crept down the stairs and opened the outside door.

"It's raining again," Melanie whispered, just as Allie saw it was and saw that Melanie had on a raincoat. "You'd better put something on. I think it's going to rain harder."

Allie nodded, pulled on oilskins and boots, and went all the way out, closing the door softly behind her.

"Thank goodness you told me that big tree's right outside your window," Melanie said, pulling Allie urgently away from the house. "I don't know how I'd have known which was your room if you hadn't."

"I don't either—but what's up?"

"Mother went into Mary Scarlett's room to close her window—she's planning to take Mary Scarlett to Bangor tomorrow—and Mary Scarlett wasn't there," Melanie said excitedly. "But there was a note, just saying 'Good-bye.'

Mother's frantic. And I just know Mary Scarlett's finally trying to run away to join Felipe. The radio says no boats can go out tonight, and anyway, Mary Scarlett doesn't know how to row or sail or anything, so someone else has to be helping her. Daddy's supposed to be coming back tonight, but I guess he won't be able to." Melanie paused for a moment, catching her breath and pushing wet hair out of her eyes. "I couldn't think of who'd be helping Mary Scarlett, but then I remembered she was talking to that cousin of yours, that boy, Dan, again yesterday, and I remembered you said it was Dan's girlfriend you saw at the fisherman's shack, and . . ."

"You're right!" Allie exclaimed, remembering Katy gesturing to Dan earlier. "I bet you're right!"

"Can you show me where the shack is?" said Melanie. "I bet they're there, waiting for the storm to end. But I've got to warn Mary Scarlett. Mother's called the police and the coast guard and everyone else she can think of. I think Mary Scarlett thought no one would miss her till morning, and she'd have all night to get away. And she didn't know there'd be a storm . . ."

Allie was already pulling Melanie through the woods toward the blueberry fields. As they ran, the rain and wind started up again, more fiercely, it seemed to Allie. Branches swept across their faces as they ran, swatting them with wet leaves and needles, and once Melanie tripped on a root and Allie caught her, holding her for a second while she got her footing. Allie kept hold of her arm then, to support her, and she thought how small and fragile Melanie seemed—but of course she really isn't, Allie realized, for she was running right along with Allie, keeping up with her. Still, she *looked* fragile, so Allie tried to keep her in the lee of her own body.

When they came out onto the ledge at the top of the island, Allie saw there was an odd yellowish tinge to the sky again, even though it was still night and the sky should have been black dark, with so many clouds. But there was a moon, and the clouds seemed to be scudding across it, now hiding it, now revealing it. She remembered that in a hurricane clouds blow into the wind, so that meant the storm was coming from the southwest now, which she figured could mean they were going to get some of the hurricane after all—and then they were across the ledge and in the woods again, stumbling and sliding on spruce needles and moss—and finally Allie saw a soft yellow glow in the distance and knew they were at the cabin.

As Allie pushed the door open, someone screamed.

Twenty

"*It's Mary Scarlett!*" Melanie shouted, running past Allie to where Dan and Katy were bending over someone lying on the bunk shelf, tossing under blankets—Mary Scarlett, for sure.

"Hang on," Katy was saying in an oddly calm voice to Mary Scarlett, but both she and Dan looked terrified. "Hang on."

Allie went closer, and saw that Katy was holding Mary Scarlett's hand, and now Melanie threw herself down beside her sister, stroking her shoulder and saying, "It's all right, Mary Scarlett, it's all right, you're safe . . ." But Melanie looked terrified, too, even though Allie thought she was trying to act brave in order to hide her fear from Mary Scarlett.

When Mary Scarlett stopped moaning and thrashing, Katy looked at her watch, and said quietly, "Ten minutes that time." She pushed back Mary Scarlett's hair, which Allie could see was soaking wet and matted. "I think that baby's some eager to come, though."

Allie looked at Dan, who'd come over to stand beside her. "She's having the baby?" Allie asked incredulously.

Dan nodded and put his arm over Allie's shoulders. She had the feeling he needed someone to hang on to near as much as she did.

Mary Scarlett moaned and struggled to sit up. "I've got to get to Felipe. I've got to."

"There's no going off here tonight," Dan said firmly, but with kindness in his voice. He gave Allie's shoulder a squeeze and went back over to the bunk. "It'd be suicide, for sure."

"This isn't exactly a sterile atmosphere," Katy said in an undertone to Dan. "And we're not exactly obstetricians. You really think we can deliver a baby?"

"Got to, I guess," Dan said grimly.

"I could get Miss Feathergill," Allie said suddenly. "She's a nurse; she'll help."

"No," said Mary Scarlett, half-sitting and wide-eyed. "She'll tell."

"She won't tell," Allie said, as sure of that as of anything. "At least not till it's safe to. I'll go get her."

She turned and ran out the door back into the storm, ignoring Dan's shout of "You come back here, Allison Ward!"

The storm's not much worse, Allie told herself, pushing her way through the woods again. But without Melanie to worry about protecting, she felt more scared than she had before. There were occasional flashes of lightning now, which she prayed wouldn't come closer when she was on the ledge, and the rain soon began pelting down harder than ever.

She fell onto the ledge more than ran onto it when she burst out of the woods, dripping wet and gasping for breath—tore her oilskin pants, too, which would make Ma mad, for they were hard to tape up. But she didn't see any lightning, and it wasn't till she got to Miss Feathergill's that she realized she'd lost her sou'wester someplace and her hair was dripping wet.

She banged on the door like one possessed, until Miss Feathergill's anxious face appeared in an upstairs window. But she must be used to being called out at night, Allie reasoned, since many times before now she'd been the only medical person on the whole island.

"Lordy, child, what's happened?" Miss Feathergill shouted down, sticking her head out the window and making a rain visor over her eyes with one hand.

"It's Mary Scarlett. Mary Scarlett Rochambeau. She's having her baby."

"I'll be right down. Come in and get dry while I get some clothes on. Door's open."

A few minutes later, Miss Feathergill, in jeans and a sweatshirt and carrying a large black bag, came down to where Allie was dripping in the hall. "You just take off those wet things and get dry," she said, pulling on her gardening boots, "while I run up to Rochambeaus' and see what's what. I thought when I saw her that time here that she was going to have a baby pretty soon, but no one said anything about it, and I didn't like to ask."

"No, you don't understand," Allie gasped. "She's not at home. She's up in the old shack. Green Mystery," she added when Miss Feathergill looked blank. And along the way, as she guided Miss Feathergill across the dark island—for there wasn't any question of Miss Feathergill's being able to find the shack in the dark in the middle of a storm—Allie explained as much as she knew about Mary Scarlett and Felipe and Mrs. Rochambeau, and Melanie and herself, too.

"I don't hold with deception, Allie Ward," Miss Feathergill grunted as they crossed the blueberry fields and plunged back into the wet woods, "even in a good cause. Although I must admit," she added, stopping a moment and gasping for breath, "this has all the earmarks of one." She clucked her tongue as she started up again, muttering about "the strangeness of some people," and she said "her own children, for pity's sake" more than once when she had breath to speak.

Melanie, her face very white, met them at the shack's door. "She screams each time she has a—a contraction, it's called," Melanie whispered to Allie when Miss Feathergill hurried over to the bunk with her black bag. "I think there's something wrong."

They all stood there silently, out of the way, while Miss

Feathergill examined Mary Scarlett, talking to her the whole time in a low voice.

"I think everything's fine," Miss Feathergill said at last. "It's just that having a baby's hard work." She patted Mary Scarlett's hand. "There, dear, you'll be better soon," she said. "And just think of the prize you'll have when it's all over."

Allie saw Mary Scarlett smile wanly.

"All right, you folks," Miss Feathergill said briskly to the rest of them. "You're all going to have to make yourselves useful. Dan, pour some of that water—assuming those gallon containers are full—into that big kettle I see on the table, and get that camp stove going. Katy, you stay by me; you're going to assist. Soon's that water's hot, we're going to wash our hands like crazy and then, Dan, you're going to heat more water. Girls—Allie, Melanie—you take one of those cardboard boxes and make a baby bed out of it. Line it with some of these blankets, and make sure there's plenty left over to wrap the baby in. See if you can cut the softest blanket into small pieces; the baby'll need washing. All right," she said, turning back to Mary Scarlett as Mary Scarlett moaned again. "All right, dear, it's okay. I'm going to give you something now to make it a little easier . . ."

Two hours later, when the storm had died down and the sun had come up into a clear blue sky, Mary Scarlett had a brand-new healthy baby boy, Melanie was an aunt, and Allie had given the baby his nickname—for as she and Melanie had washed him, she'd said, "He's slippery as a minnow." Mary Scarlett had laughed happily, taking him from them, and said, "That's what I'll call him. Not Felipe José Samuel Gonzales, but Minnow. My little island Minnow."

Twenty-one

"*Now then,*" said Miss Feath- ergill, taking charge while Mary Scarlett slept, with Min- now in his box next to her, "we have to have a plan." She looked at Dan and Katy. "You must've had some plan to be- gin with, fixing this old place up as you did."

"What we were going to do," said Dan, "was keep Mary Scarlett here for a couple of days after she left her house till everyone stopped looking for her, and . . ."

"Assuming no one found her," Miss Feathergill inter- rupted. "Quite an assumption, I'd say."

"It was all we could think of," said Katy. "Of course we didn't know the baby was going to come early. Anyway, we knew she couldn't go off on the mailboat, for everyone would see her, so we were going to take her in Dan's boat, soon as suspicion died down enough."

"And take her where?"

"To Spruce Harbor, where she was going to call Felipe and he was going to come and get her."

"Does that mean that poor boy is waiting and wondering what's gone wrong?"

Katy shook her head. "Not exactly. It got all spoiled when Mrs. Rochambeau announced yesterday she was taking Mary Scarlett to Bangor today. Everything had to be speeded up . . ."

". . . and we'd have taken her right off," Dan said, "if it hadn't been for the storm."

"And the baby," Katy added.

"I see," said Miss Feathergill, rather grimly, Allie thought. "So *now* what's the plan?"

"There isn't one," Katy admitted, and Dan shrugged sheepishly.

"I think," Allie said, "that we ought to take Mary Scarlett and Minnow to the mainland today and call Felipe and have him come and get her."

"Yes," said Melanie.

"But *I* think," said Miss Feathergill, "that this whole business has gone far enough. Yes, Mary Scarlett needs to go to Felipe, if that's what both she and Felipe want, but someone's got to tell her parents, who no doubt are worried sick over where she is . . ."

"Mad's more likely," Melanie muttered.

". . . and I'd feel better if a doctor checked both her and the baby over soon as possible."

"Maybe we should get her to the mainland first, though," said Katy. "Before we say anything to her mother."

"If Mother sees that baby," said Melanie, "she'll take him away from her and give him to a social worker. That's what she said she was going to do."

"Yes," said Miss Feathergill, thoughtfully. "Allie did mention that. But I'm not at all sure she could do that without Mary Scarlett's agreeing to it."

"I don't think Mary Scarlett would agree," Melanie said, looking at her sleeping sister. "Not after having Minnow and seeing him and everything. But Mother can be pretty fierce."

"Well, anyway," Dan said impatiently, "we've got to get her to the mainland. How about I go see if my boat made it through the storm, and if she did, I'll take Mary Scarlett and the baby off right away and get them to Doc Coolidge. Then we can tell Mrs. R."

"Mmmm," said Miss Feathergill. "I suppose that might work."

"I'll just bring my boat around here, then," said Dan. "If I can. Some boat, anyway. Allie, you awake enough to be my crew?"

"Sure am," Allie said eagerly.

So Dan and Allie walked across the island once more and, after stopping quickly to tell their respective parents what was going on, found that Dan's small sloop had weathered the storm just fine. There was still plenty of wind, so they sailed around to the back of the island, sometimes with Allie at the tiller, and anchored the sloop as close in as they dared.

But then, just as they were climbing into the dinghy to go ashore and get the others, a coast guard boat hailed them.

"Damn!" Dan said under his breath.

"You seen a young girl, long blond hair, anyplace, maybe in a boat?" shouted an officer.

"No!" Allie shouted back, but Dan shouted, "Yes, sir. She's safe in the old fish shack, and she's doing just fine, right as rain. No need to worry."

"That was some stupid!" Allie snapped angrily. "Why'd you say that?"

"Because it's true, Allie. Doesn't do to argue with the coast guard. Most of 'em's good folks. If they want to know more, we'll explain more, too. It'll be okay."

"But her mother . . ."

"Allie, her mother's going to know someday about this baby."

"Sooner than someday," Allie said, still angry—for the coastguardsman had just helped a tall blond woman into his dinghy and now he was rowing to shore with the woman—Mrs. Rochambeau—sitting tensely in the bow, her mouth, without its usual pink lipstick, set in a thin, tight line.

"Oh, Lordy!" Dan said, rowing harder. "I didn't count on that."

"If you hadn't said anything, it wouldn't have happened, either," Allie muttered. "You've just gone and spoiled the whole thing, that's what you've done."

"Too late to take back what I said now." Dan beached his dinghy scant moments after the coastguardsman beached his.

Mrs. Rochambeau stepped out. "You!" she said, looking from Allie to Dan and back to Allie. "I should have known you'd be up to something. Where is my daughter?"

"She's safe," Dan said, "and sound, but I'm not real sure that she wants . . ."

"Take me to her," Mrs. Rochambeau ordered imperiously. Then, to Allie's surprise, her voice quavered and she asked, "Is she really all right?"

"Yes, she really is," Allie said.

"What's going on?" the coastguardsman asked, and Dan took him aside and started explaining in a low voice. That left Allie to guide Mrs. Rochambeau over the rocks and through the woods to the shack. "She's really fine," Allie said. "Honest."

"I—was so worried," Mrs. Rochambeau said softly, as if to herself. Then she tripped on a root and clutched Allie for support. Allie felt some weird, holding up the one person in the whole world whom she hated, and who she figured hated her, too. "I didn't know . . ." Mrs. Rochambeau said over and over again. "I didn't know she was really so . . ."

Allie was surprised to see that Mrs. Rochambeau was almost sobbing, at least her breath was coming in short, staccato gasps, and she remembered what Daddy had said about people's troubles sometimes turning them mean and near crazy.

Mrs. Rochambeau was still muttering as if Allie weren't there. Allie was almost embarrassed, catching what seemed to be private fragments through the woman's sobs: "I was so worried . . . That boy is so . . . I can't imagine . . . poor child . . . I didn't know . . ."

Then they reached the door of the shack and Mrs. Rochambeau let go of Allie's arm. Trembling, she went toward the bunk.

Melanie gasped and moved out of her mother's way, to Allie.

"She seems sorry," Allie whispered. "She really does."

"Mary Scarlett?" Mrs. Rochambeau whispered; she'd completely ignored Melanie. "Oh, God! Are you—are you all right?"

Mary Scarlett opened her eyes. "Go away," she said coldly. "Please leave me alone. I don't want to see you anymore. Not ever."

Allie saw Mary Scarlett's eyes close again, and saw Dan and Katy and Miss Feathergill go outside, beckoning to Allie and Melanie, as if they thought whatever was going to happen next should be private, just between Mrs. Rochambeau and Mary Scarlett. But Allie knew she wasn't about to leave Melanie there alone, and Melanie didn't look any more likely to move than one of those granite boulders in the woods near the blueberry fields.

Melanie slipped her hand into Allie's.

Mrs. Rochambeau bowed her head. "Perhaps I was foolish," she said softly. "But that—that foreign boy is just not—not suitable, Mary Scarlett. It would really be best for everyone, for the baby, too, if you gave . . ."

There was a choked cry of "No!" from Mary Scarlett, who reached down and grabbed the edge of Minnow's box, as if to protect him.

Mrs. Rochambeau bent down and said something Allie couldn't hear. Then she straightened up and in almost her old voice said, "Now please, please, come home and let's talk about this sensibly."

Mary Scarlett struggled to sit, and she picked Minnow up out of his box and held him close. "No," she said. "It's too late to talk. It's too late. You don't want us, Felipe and me and our baby. You don't think Felipe's good enough, and I don't want you to . . ."

Mrs. Rochambeau was about to get really mad, Allie could tell. Melanie's hand gripped hers tightly and through it she could feel Melanie shaking.

So Allie went over to the bunk, leaned over, and took Minnow gently from Mary Scarlett. She pulled back his blankets a little so his tiny face, still red, showed. "Look, both of you," she said. "This is Felipe José Samuel Gonzales. Minnow. And he's both of yours. He's your grandson, Mrs. Rochambeau. I know you want to give him to someone else, and I guess someone really nice might adopt him and he might be happy with them, but that seems a waste since he's already got a family." She faced Mrs. Rochambeau. "He's your *grandson*," she said again. "Don't you want to hold him?"

Mrs. Rochambeau stared at the baby for a minute. Allie held her breath as the woman's face softened. But then Mrs. Rochambeau turned away abruptly and strode to the door, rushing past Allie and Melanie—and nearly colliding with two damp, bedraggled figures who were pushing their way in, closely followed by Miss Feathergill, Dan, and Katy.

"Daddy!" Melanie cried just as Allie recognized him and, much to her surprise, Johnny Buttons.

Allie remembered Melanie's saying that her father was due back the night of the storm—but how on earth had he managed to get across to the island when no boats were going out? And she remembered that Miss Feathergill had said Johnny had shown her the shack last year, so of course he knew where it was. But how had Mr. Rochambeau connected with him? And how had Johnny known to lead Mr. Rochambeau to the shack?

Mr. Rochambeau thrust his wife aside, patted Melanie's shoulder briefly, and went quickly to Mary Scarlett. "Are you all right?" he asked, bending over the bunk. "Honey, are you . . . ?"

Mary Scarlett clung to him. "Don't let her take my baby!" she sobbed. "Don't let her!"

"I won't, sweetheart." Mr. Rochambeau took Minnow from Allie and sat with him on the edge of the bunk, as if he and Mary Scarlett and Minnow were alone in a real house somewhere, without anyone else around. "What a fine little boy," he said softly. "He looks a lot like you, Mary Scarlett."

Allie saw Mary Scarlett smile through her tears. "He's got Felipe's eyes," Mary Scarlett said, "and yours and Melanie's hands, I think. Oh, Daddy, Felipe has the most beautiful eyes!"

"I'm sure he has," Mr. Rochambeau said. "And as soon as we get you and the baby home, we'll call Felipe so he can come and get you. And," he went on, looking severely at his wife, who was huddled by the door near Miss Feathergill, Dan, and Katy, "as soon as he comes, we'll see about you two getting married, which should have happened months ago. Thanks to Mr. Buttons here, I found you just in time."

"But how . . ." Allie began.

"Dan told Johnny where he was going," Katy explained, "and what he and I were planning. And . . ."

Dan took up the story. "I figured someone should know in case something happened, and I knew Johnny was the only person who wouldn't say anything unless something bad did happen."

"Very sensible," Miss Feathergill said, and she patted Dan's arm.

"It took me longer than usual to get to Spruce Harbor last night because of the storm," Mr. Rochambeau explained. "But when I got there early this morning and called the house, Cookie was almost hysterical about no one's being home. I managed to find someone to bring me across to the island—and as soon as I got to the dock, I started asking people if they'd seen my family. Johnny said something that sounded like he knew and he led me here."

Johnny, who had been watching and listening carefully, went to Allie's side. "Bay-bee," he said, putting out a finger and very gently brushing Minnow's face. He looked back pointedly at Mrs. Rochambeau. "Luck-ee bay-bee." He pointed to himself and said, "Oh-pan. No ma." He pointed again to Minnow—"No oh-pan"—and then to Mary Scarlett and Mr. and Mrs. Rochambeau in turn. "Ma. Gan-pa. Gam-ma. Luck-ee bay-bee."

Mrs. Rochambeau sniffed loudly. "What on earth is he trying to say?"

"He's saying," Allie answered around the lump in her throat, "that he's an orphan and doesn't have a mother. And that Minnow's a lucky baby because he's not an orphan. He has a mother and a grandfather and a grandmother. And"—she smiled at Melanie—"he's got an aunt, too." She looked straight at Mrs. Rochambeau. "He's also got a father," she said, not caring if she was being rude. "Felipe José Samuel Gonzales Minnow has got a whole family all his own."

The next day, Felipe arrived on the mailboat, and the day after that, he and Mary Scarlett and Minnow and Mr. Rochambeau prepared to go off on it again, bound for Spruce Harbor and Dr. Coolidge and then probably Bangor so that Mary Scarlett and Felipe could go to city hall or a justice of the peace and get married. Just about everyone went to see them off, and Johnny Buttons, standing on the dock near Allie and Melanie, played "Rock-A-Bye Baby" softly on his comb as Mary Scarlett carried Minnow toward the mailboat.

Mary Scarlett stopped in front of Johnny. "Thank you," she said. "For everything."

Felipe reached out and grasped Johnny's hand, shaking it, and Johnny's smile was almost wide enough to cover his whole face.

"Felipe's so perfect," Melanie said to Allie when the boat had left. "And guess what? Daddy's making Mother give them a real wedding in Boston. Mother actually held Minnow for a few minutes last night, and she even laughed at a funny story Felipe told. I think she might be beginning to like him. It's hard not to."

Allie just smiled, for she didn't trust Mrs. Rochambeau much, even though she did feel sort of sorry for her, if only because she was missing so much by being mean to people. She knew she should be grateful that Mrs. Rochambeau had told Melanie she could see Allie all she wanted, but she bet Mr. Rochambeau had made her do that, too, just like the wedding.

It wasn't long until Labor Day and the end of summer, but every day till then, Allie went up to the big white house after working in the pie shop, or Melanie came down to Allie's house, and they made up for all the time they'd lost, and as far as Allie knew, Mrs. Rochambeau didn't say a word anymore against anyone who lived on the island. Right before Labor Day Miss Feathergill went back to Boston, saying as she always did that next year she'd move to the island full-time for sure. Allie's daddy went out regularly on the *Cindy One* with Dan, and said that since Allie'd shown herself to be so brave in the storm she could come, too, sometimes, on weekends, and show them what she could do. He didn't promise any more than that, but Allie felt wicked hopeful. Come Labor Day, Ma and Allie closed up the pie shop and took in the sign, and Ma hugged Allie hard, saying, "We made it, Allie, didn't we, thanks to your help. No need for any of that talk of moving now!"

Then school started. Sarah and Matthew came home from Aunt Eulalie's, and Allie and Todd and Michael glared at each other across their upstairs classroom. The Corrigans went home, and Betsy and Deirdre cried as they left. On the Saturday after Labor Day (for Melanie's private school opened late), Mrs. Rochambeau and Melanie drove down to the dock and Allie got permission to leave school for an hour in order to say good-bye.

"I'll write you long letters," Melanie said tearfully. "I promise."

"And I'll write you long letters back," Allie said around the lump in her throat. "And if your mother doesn't want to come back next summer, maybe you can come anyway and visit me."

"Maybe," said Melanie. "Or maybe you could come visit me."

"I just might," Allie said, thinking, if Miss Feathergill keeps going off-island to Boston, there must be something worth seeing there.

And if Melanie'll be there . . .

The mailboat whistled and Mrs. Rochambeau, who was already aboard, called out, "Melanie, come along, dear, now."

Melanie gave Allie a long look and a quick hug and then, calling "Friends forever!" jumped aboard.

"Friends forever!" Allie called back.

She watched the mailboat sail away till her eyes were too blurred with tears to see it anymore.

But then she looked down at the bracelet Melanie had made for her, which she still always wore. She touched it gently, blinked back her tears, and started planning her first letter as she walked back up the hill to school.